The Keeper
by
Andrew Hawthorne

Dedications

This book is dedicated to my second grandson, Andrew who was born just a few days after I finished the first draft of this book.

I should like to take this opportunity to thank my good friend David Rooney who proof read the book and hopefully found all my typos.

Finally, thanks to everyone who bought my first book and gave such positive reviews without which I doubt if I would have had the confidence to continue writing and complete this book.

Chapter One

When she opened her eyes there was only darkness. She lay very still on the small bed, terrified to move. Anne had no idea how she had ended up there and no idea how long she had been asleep. As her eyes slowly adjusted to the darkness she thought she could see the outline of what appeared to be a chair in the opposite corner of the room. There was a smell of dampness in the air, not of rotting wood but more earthy, like a damp basement might smell. She decided to sit up slowly and take a better look at her surroundings. As she did this, the small bed on which she was sitting creaked and groaned from the shift in her body weight. She slowly twisted her body around towards the edge of the bed and placed her feet on the cold damp floor. *Shoes! Where are my shoes?*

She began to panic and shouted, "Hello…hello… is there anyone there?   Can anyone hear me?"

There was no response. She sat there listening to the silence, trying to control her breathing which was getting heavier and heavier as her heart began to race with fear.

After a few minutes her heart rate began to slow down as the adrenalin in her veins gradually dissipated. She knew all about how the human body reacted to fear; preparing itself for fight or flight. She had studied biology at high school but having some knowledge of how the human body works did not help her to cope with her current predicament as she was clearly unable to fight or run. She decided to get up and carefully searched around the small room to see if she could find a door or a way out. As she got to her feet she felt a little woozy. She steadied herself, stretched out her arms and extended her fingers tentatively feeling her way all around the bed until she touched the wall. She continued to feel her way around the wall until she felt the door frame. She reached for the door handle hoping that she would be able to make her way out of the small room. The handle did turn a little but when she pulled gently at the door nothing happened. It was locked. The panic began to return and she decided to bang on the door and shout for help. After a few minutes of extreme effort she stopped trying, her hands were sore and her knuckles had started to bleed. She sat down on the hard cold floor with her back against the door and started to weep.

As she sat there crying she began to think about what could have happened to her. All she could remember was that she had been on a night out with some friends in Glasgow and after a few drinks had started to feel unwell so she decided to go home early. The last thing she actually remembered was waiting for a bus at her usual bus stop outside the kebab shop on Argyle Street and then there was nothing. *Had she been drugged?* That was the only explanation she could think of that made any sense. At first she had blamed the feeling of sickness on the alcohol but had not even considered the possibility of her drink being tampered with. Her Dad had warned her several times about the so-called rape drugs and she had always been very careful with her drinks, up until now. *Shit! Had she been raped while asleep?* She certainly didn't feel like she had – consensual or otherwise. She wasn't promiscuous or anything like it but she knew what it felt like after the event and she was sure that she hadn't. *So if her abductor did not want her for sex then what did he want?* Her heart sank as another thought entered her head. *Oh God, did he want to kill her?* Then logic kicked in – if he wanted to kill her then why was she still alive. Then an even worse thought entered her head. *Oh shit, did he want her to be awake when he killed her, was he going to torture her first or did he want to see her die slowly. What sort of animal was he?* Her mind raced along with her increasing heart rate as the reality of her situation slowly began to sink to the pit in the bottom of her stomach, like an immoveable rock.

Suddenly there was the creaking sound of a door opening in the distance and her heart almost jumped out of her chest. She got up from her seated position on the floor and threw herself in the direction of the bed. She sat bolt upright on the bed and faced the door. She heard a small click, a light switch, and then saw shards of light appear around the edges of the door, illuminating it so it appeared almost mystical. She heard a few footsteps and then a bolt being slid open on the other side of the door, then another and another. *Three bolts, she thought. I'm never going to get that door opened from the inside.*

She suddenly thought that this might be her only chance to get free. She would lunge at her abductor as soon as the door was opened wide enough for her to get by, push him out of the way and make a run for it. *Fight or flight? It was a no brainer. She would run as fast as she could for as long as she could until every drop of adrenalin was drained from her system.*

She stood up, getting ready to spring at him. He wouldn't be expecting this so she would catch him off guard. As the door opened inwards towards her she leapt straight at the small but sturdy figure standing in the doorway. However, she had not taken into account the impact of the bright lights on her ability to see clearly and instinctively she closed her eyes to shield them, misjudged the run and hit the edge of the half opened door, head first, hard and fast. She stumbled and fell back onto the bed screaming with agonising pain, holding her head which was now thumping as the blood rushed through her veins but worse still, it was bleeding. The man who had been standing at the doorway watching her antics with bemusement came all the way into the room, closed the door behind him and turned on the lights. He had short dark hair, a large forehead, heavy eyebrows over very dark brown eyes which were deep inset into his skull. The shape of his head and face reminded her of images she had seen of early cave men.

"Well, that wasn't very clever was it?" he said and started to laugh.

Her anger overtook her fear. "Who are you and what do you want? You, you fucking arsehole!"

"Swearing is against the rules, Anne," he said. "But as I haven't had the chance to explain the rules yet I'll let it go this time."

Anne froze. "How do you know my name?" she asked.

"Oh, I know a lot more than that about you, *Anne Duncan.* You see, your presence here is no accident."

This sent a chill right through her spine. "What do you want with me?" she asked again, this time with less aggression and anger.

He smiled and said "Oh, that's easy. I want to *keep* you."

"Keep me! What do you mean?"

"Precisely that, you are my prisoner and you belong to me now," he replied offhandedly.

He looked at the wound on her head and grimaced. "I'll go and get the first aid kit," he said as he moved towards the door, keeping an eye on her to make sure she wasn't about to attempt another escape.

Anne watched him close the door and heard him slide the three bolts back into place. She sat there silently, a bit sore and a bit confused. He returned within a few minutes with the kit and immediately set about gently cleaning her wounds and then he wrapped a bandage all the way around the top of her head, clamping her matted hair firmly against her wounded scalp.

"You can clean the rest of the blood off your hands and face over there at the sink," he said, pointing to the opposite corner of the room.

She hadn't noticed the small table with a small basin full of water at the back of the room. There was also a large bucket with a lid underneath it; she guessed this must be her makeshift toilet as there was nothing else in the room! She stood up slowly, pushing herself up with both hands, wobbled a little and then went over to the sink and washed and dried herself with a small white towel which was hanging on the rail next to the sink and then returned to the bed.

"That's better, now we can have a civilised chat," he said and sat on the little chair opposite the bed.

"Civilised! You must be joking, you…you…fucking Neanderthal!" Anne exclaimed. "You drug me and lock me up in this godforsaken hell hole and then call this civilised! You are off your fucking…."

"Ah, ah, no swearing! You were warned and now I'm going to have to punish you."

"Punish me, what do you mean. What are you going to do?" she asked, suddenly concerned that she had gone too far.

"It's not what I'm going to do," he said calmly. "It's what I'm not going to do."

"What do you mean? That doesn't make any sense."

He looked at her, enjoying her confusion. "For a start, I'm not going to bring you anything to eat tonight!"

"Fine by me. I wouldn't eat anything you give me anyway," she said sneeringly.

"Well, we'll see how you feel about that after a few days without any food, won't we."

"Huh, I won't be here that long. The police will be looking for me as we speak and will soon find this place."

"Oh they will, will they? I wouldn't build my hopes up on that happening any time soon. You see the Police aren't very interested in missing persons at the moment. People can go missing for days, months even and they don't really care. But don't worry I'll keep you informed of any news, providing you stick to the rules, of course!"

"Oh, yes of course, the rules. No swearing, are there any others that I should know about?"

"Just a few, no shouting, no violence, including self harming, and don't try to escape. If you follow the rules we will get on famously and if you please me, I will reward you."

"Please you, if you think I'm going to…"

"Stop! I'm not interested in having sex with you if that's what you're thinking. I don't want to harm you Anne. I will look after you providing you follow the rules. You see, I want to understand what makes you tick, I want to find out who you really are? Treat it like a bit of a social experiment. Can you do that?"

"So, all I need to do is talk to you and you won't harm me?"

"Yes, exactly!"

He smiled at her and sat down on the small chair. "Now Anne, let's start again shall we? Tell me about your childhood."

"My childhood! I don't even know your name!"

"Oh I'm sorry, how rude of me. You can call me…Robert."

"So, that's not your real name then?"

"Of course not, I'm not that stupid! Anyway, my name is not important. So, Anne, tell me about your childhood," he pressed, eager to explore her past.

Anne hesitated while she considered what to do next. Her main concern right now was to keep herself safe. *Even though 'Robert' had said he would not harm her, how could she trust him?* She needed more time to think about what to do, so she decided to go along with his little game for now. "Okay, where do you want me to start?"

His eyes lit up with delight. "What was your first childhood memory?"

"Hmm, oh yeah, my earliest childhood memory is being at home with my Mum and Dad in our first house in Maryhill. I can remember playing with my Dad in the garden in the summertime. I must have been about three or four years old. I remember one day in particular when Mum was taken into hospital and Dad had to look after me. I found out later that Mum had cancer." Anne suddenly realised that she was giving him too much personal information and stopped herself. "Anyway, that's my first memory."

"What type of cancer?" he asked.

"None of your business! I've said too much already."

"Okay, so what happened when your Mum was diagnosed? Who looked after you?"

"My Dad, of course."

"Yes, but he must have had some help when your Mum was ill?"

"I remember my gran coming round for a while."

"Funny that, isn't it?"

"What, my gran coming round?"

"No, that our earliest memories tend to be sad or traumatic ones. I'm fascinated by how the human brain works."

She sat there quietly contemplating his observation. "I hadn't really thought about it before."

"Tell me about your earliest happy memory?" he asked.

"Oh that's easy," she said. "When Mum was finally given the all clear by the doctors, Dad threw a big party and invited the whole family around to the house. I was just pleased that my mum was well again," said Anne, wiping a small tear from the corner of her right eye. The memory was still very vivid and even now it affected her.

Chapter Two

Catherine Duncan woke up just after 8.15 a.m. Her husband George was still sleeping so she got up quietly and went downstairs into the kitchen and put on the kettle. She looked around and thought that the kitchen looked remarkably tidy given that Anne had been out on the town last night. Normally when her daughter came home after drinking she would raid the fridge and there would be plenty of evidence left lying around the kitchen but today there was nothing. *Strange, she thought.*

She went back upstairs to check that Anne was in her bed only to find the bed fully made up and no evidence of Anne coming home; there were no clothes dumped on the floor in a heap. She immediately went next door. "George, wake up, Anne didn't come home last night."

"Eh, what," he said, still half a sleep. He sat up slowly and looked at the clock and sighed; he liked to sleep in a little bit longer than usual on Sunday. "What's the matter Cathy?"

Cathy sighed at having to repeat herself. "Anne didn't come home last night. She's not been in her bed all night."

"Well, she might have stayed over at a friend's house. Have you checked the phone for any messages?"

"What? No, I didn't think of that. That'll be it. Where's my phone? Cathy found her phone which was sitting on her bedside table and checked for messages. "Nothing!"

"What about the landline? She might have left a message on the answering machine." Cathy went downstairs to check the answering machine.

George followed Cathy downstairs. The small black machine sat in the corner of the room, flashing its green light to indicate that there was a message waiting. The machine had been programmed to 'do not disturb' after midnight and therefore any calls after that point went straight to the answer machine. Anne pressed the button to hear the stored messages.

"*Hi Anne, it's Jean. I tried your mobile and got no reply. Just checking that you got home alright and feel a bit better. You certainly didn't look that well when you left. Call me in the morning when you feel up to it.*"

Cathy turned and looked at George who immediately said, "Call Jean and ask her what time Anne left the pub?"

Cathy used the auto-redial function on the telephone handset to call Jean back but there was no response and then Jean's voicemail message kicked in. Cathy left a brief message for Jean to call her back as soon as possible and hung up. "She's probably still asleep and has her phone turned off," said Cathy. "I'm going round to Jean's house to wake her up. I don't think we should wait."

"Okay, let's both get dressed and I'll come with you," said George, who was now just as concerned as Cathy. He now had a very bad feeling about this.

The Duncans left the house as soon as they were dressed and decided to take the car to save some time. Jean McArthur only lived a few streets away so it only took a few minutes to get there. Jean and Anne had been friends since nursery and were still very close friends. Most of their other friends had moved out of the area but they still kept in touch with each other via WhatsApp. Jean's parents used to live next door to the Duncans' house but both had died in a tragic car accident two years ago and their house had been sold and the equity shared equally between their two children, Jean and her younger brother Gordon. Jean had bought an ex council house in Maryhill with her share but

Gordon was keen to move out of the area and bought a one-bedroomed flat in Anderston.

As soon as the car came to a stop Catherine jumped out, slammed the door and ran towards the entrance to Jean's close. By the time George got out the car, Cathy was out of sight. He entered the small narrow close and saw Cathy standing at Jean's door with her finger on the doorbell.

"There's no answer," said Cathy as she saw George approach.

"Are you sure the bell's working? Rattle the letterbox, just in case," he said pointing to the small silver letter box half way down the dark blue door.

Cathy rattled the letterbox. They waited for a few seconds and then George stood forward and gave the letterbox a louder rattle. He bent down to try and look through the letterbox just as Jean opened the door. She was wearing red tartan pyjamas underneath a pink dressing robe. Her hair was ruffled, her eyes were half closed; it was clear she had just got out of bed.

"Hello Jean, sorry to bother you this early but Anne didn't come home last night and…"

"What? Oh my God! You better come in," said Jean suddenly awake with the news.

They followed Jean into her small living room and sat down. "I feel terrible. I knew I should have went home with Anne but she insisted that she'd be fine. She said she was just feeling a bit under the weather. I'm sorry. Really I am!"

"It's alright Jean, nobody's blaming you," said Cathy. "I think we should call the Police though as this is not like Anne at all."

"I agree," said George.

"You can call from here if you want and use my landline. They'll probably want to speak to me anyway as I was one of the last persons to see her."

"Good idea Jean, I'll call them now", said George,

"I'll go and get dressed. "Feel free to make some tea or coffee," said Jean heading to the door.

George made the phone call and then they both waited patiently for the Police to arrive. Cathy's stomach was churning and she felt physically sick. This was surreal. It was the sort of thing you see on the news or read about in the newspapers and pray will never happen to you or someone you love. Cathy closed her eyes and prayed that it was all one big misunderstanding and that her daughter would call her on her mobile. The door bell went and Cathy jumped out of her chair and went to the door. Jean came down the stairs only to find that Cathy had already invited the two police officers into the narrow hallway. Cathy led them into the living room followed by Jean. Once everyone was seated the older of the two policemen spoke first.

"Good morning, my name is Constable Downie and this is Constable Ross, I understand you have reported a missing person. Was it you who made the call to the station Mr..?"

"Duncan, George Duncan." Constable Downie opened a small electronic pad and started typing the details into the machine.

"So you use electronic note pads these days?" said Cathy admiring the small electronic device.

Yes, we have all the mod cons now. And you must be Mrs Duncan? Is that correct?"

"Yes, Catherine Duncan, but you can call me Cathy."

"Thank you Cathy." He looked across the room to where Jean was sitting. "And you are?

"Jean McArthur, I'm a friend of Anne's. Well, she's my best friend. I've known her for years."

"Okay, now that we all know each other, I'll need to take a statement from each of you. To save some time, Constable Ross will take your statement Jean. According to the phone call to the station you were the last person to see Anne before she went missing, is that correct?"

"Yes, but there were a few others with us in the night club."

"That's fine, if you give all the details to Constable Ross then we can contact the others in due course."

PC Ross stood up. "Can we use your kitchen, Jean?"

"What? Oh, yes, sure, this way."

As soon as Jean left the room PC Downie began to speak. "Now, can I have your full address please?"

"I've already given the officer at the station our address," said George rather abrasively.

"Yes, I know, but I need to record all the information on the note pad and take a formal statement."

"What do you mean, a formal statement, you don't think we had anything to do with Anne's disappearance, do you? And that's another thing. Why are you doing this? I was expecting CID to be there."

"George!" said Cathy sharply. "That's enough. Let the policeman do his job."

"No, it's okay Mrs Duncan, I mean Cathy, I'm sorry but it's just Police protocol, that's all. Now don't worry, once we have taken your initial statements a detective will review the case and decide what needs to be done so if I can start with you, Mr Duncan. When was the last time you saw your daughter, Anne?"

"I think it was about 9.15 last night. I was sitting watching the telly when Anne popped her head round the door and told me she was going out with Jean and few of their friends."

"Did she say where she was going?"

"No, I assumed she was going into the town."

"For the record I take it you mean the city – Glasgow?"

"Yes, the City of Glasgow but don't ask me which pub or clubs they go to."

"That's fine. Ms McArthur can tell us that. Can you remember what Anne was wearing when she left the house?"

"Sorry, I can't remember."

"I can," said Cathy interrupting the conversation. "She was wearing a dark blue party dress with a grey and red checked coat and black shoes with a medium heal."

"Thanks Mrs Duncan. If you don't mind I'm taking your husband's statement at the moment. "You'll get your opportunity to speak in a few minutes."

George could tell that Cathy was livid with the young policeman and deliberately avoided making eye contact with her.

"Mr Duncan, can you remember if your daughter was wearing any jewellery when she left the house?"

"I assume she was but I really can't remember. Sorry, I'm not very observant."

"No. it's fine. How tall is Anne?"

"Just a few inches shorter than me. I'd say about 5 feet 6 inches." He looked at Cathy for confirmation and she nodded her head in agreement.

"And build, was she slim, medium or...?"

"Eh, I would say medium." And again Cathy nodded in agreement.

"Oh, and does Anne have a boyfriend at the moment?"

"No, she did go with a lad a while ago but she dumped him and good riddance, I never liked him anyway."

"What was his name?"

"Brian Davidson," George replied, expressing his disapproval again.

"And where does Brian live?"

"Somewhere near Yoker, I think, not sure really. You don't think Brian has got anything to do with this, do you?"

"I'm just gathering all relevant information at the moment Mr Duncan. Let's not jump to any conclusions yet," said PC Downie.

"Alright, I'm going to need a recent photograph of your daughter. Is that okay?"

"Of course, I'm sure we'll have something suitable back home."

"Okay Mrs Duncan, I'll take your statement now."

George could see Cathy was still raging. She turned toward the Constable and just nodded. The police officer repeated the same set of questions that had been asked of Mr Duncan. Cathy was able to provide more details of clothing and described in some detail the blue earrings that Anne was wearing before she went missing. PC Downie finished taking the statement and then went through to the kitchen to see how his colleague was doing. It was clear from the conversation taking place when he entered that they had finished and were now just having a casual chat. On seeing his colleague enter the room, PC Ross stopped talking and got to his feet. "You'll never guess, but me and Jean went to the same high school. I was in the year above her at school and the chances are that I'll recognise Anne when I see a photograph of her."

"We can follow Mr and Mrs Duncan back to their place to get a recent photograph," said PC Downie signalling to his colleague to follow him out.

"You don't need to do that," said Jean. "I've got a recent photo on my phone. In fact I might have one from last night. I remember taking a few photos before Anne left so with any luck you can use it." Jean quickly scrolled through her phone and found one. "Will this one do?"

The two police officers looked at the photograph and both nodded simultaneously. "That's perfect," PC Ross replied. "But I don't remember Anne from school. Has she changed much?"

Before she could reply PC Downie interrupted the conversation. "Can you send the photo to me?" he asked and gave her his mobile number.

Jean happily agreed and sent the photo to the police officer who checked that he had received it and promptly went back through to the living room where Mr and Mrs Duncan were sitting rather impatiently.

"Are you happy for us to use this photograph of your daughter? asked PC Downie.

Jean took it last night so it's very recent and more importantly Anne is wearing the same clothing as she was when she went missing. It could be very useful."

Cathy stood up first. Looked at the photograph and nodded. George followed her and also gave his approval.

"Thanks, we'll circulate it to all local police offices first, put it out on social media, etc., if that's okay with you and then take it from there."

They both nodded in agreement. "So what happens now?" asked Cathy, her anxiety starting to build again.

"We'll go back to the station, file the report and then we'll put an alert out to all police officers in the area to look out for your daughter. They'll get a description and a copy of the photo. We'll also contact all local hospitals just in case she's taken not well and someone has taken her there. It's likely that one of our detectives will want to speak to you as they might have some more questions so it's important that you stay at home in case they call you. Is that okay? And of course, if we find her we'll let you know as soon as possible."

"Thank you PC, eh ...?" said George trying hard to remember the young policeman's name.

"It's Downie, PC Downie and PC Ross," he said smiling.

"Of course, sorry and thank you again."

"It's not a problem. We'll be in touch, bye for now," said PC Downie and he left the room.

George looked at Cathy who looked like she was about to cry and then did. He went over to her and gave her a hug. "It'll be alright love. The Police will find her. I'm sure they will."

Chapter Three

The interview with Andrew McLaren, who was being held on suspicion of beating up his partner was going to plan. Detective Inspector Claire Redding and Detective Sergeant Brian O'Neill had a raft of evidence which they were slowly releasing to McLaren and his solicitor, Matilda Baker of Stein, McLeod and Partners. The plan was to overwhelm the man slowly and gradually coerce him into confessing or at least persuade his solicitor that there was absolutely no chance of getting him off. They began by summarising his previous convictions of assault, grievous bodily harm and numerous counts of breach of the peace, just in case McLaren hadn't fully briefed the young solicitor, who up until now had not made any contribution to the interview.

DI Redding was on a roll and really enjoying the obvious pain of each evidential dagger that she metaphorically stuck into McLaren. She decided to go for the jugular and use the forensic evidence which she had deliberately kept to last.

"Mr McLaren, I shouldn't need to remind you that it is absolutely pointless denying these charges. Your partner, Shona McAllister, has provided a full statement against you, which has been corroborated by her daughter Emma. Furthermore, you were arrested at the scene of the crime in a drunken stupor, covered in blood. DI Redding paused for a moment and put a clear plastic bag containing a blue, blood stained, shirt in front of McLaren.

"Do you recognise this shirt?" she asked, keeping eye contact with McLaren. He didn't blink and said, "No comment."

"Well for your information this is the shirt you were wearing when you were arrested by two of our officers, who have also provided a statement which will be used against you in court." She turned and looked at the young solicitor and then back to McLaren. "Oh, and you'll never guess what our forensic team found when we tested some samples of blood and hairs taken from this shirt that Mr McLaren was wearing when we found him."

DS O'Neill took this opening as his cue and placed a thin brown folder in front of Ms Baker and opened it to reveal a copy of the forensic report.

"Mr McLaren, the blood on your shirt belongs to your partner, the DNA was a perfect match. And what's more we also took samples of blood found on your hands and guess what?" she said sarcastically. "It was your partner's blood. So, as you can see, we have more than enough evidence to persuade even the most lenient of juries that you are guilty of committing Grievous Bodily Harm. That and the fact that you have a long history of violence against women should be more than enough to lock you up for a very long time. Do you have anything to say for the record?" She paused for a few seconds to give McLaren time to take in his situation. Silence.

"No? Well, can you explain how the blood was found on your shirt and hands?" Again silence. McLaren just sat there, said nothing and stared at the wall behind DI Redding.

"Ok. Here's what we are going to do. I'm going to give you a few minutes alone with Ms Baker here and hopefully she can advise you on the best course of action. Interview suspended at 11.15 am. DS O'Neill and DI Redding leaving the room."

DI Redding switched off the recording device and DS O'Neill removed the plastic evidence bag but left the forensic report open for the solicitor to read. He had been here before and knew exactly what was going to happen. McLaren would attempt to persuade his solicitor that he's innocent and this is all a set up by the big bad Police, just like what happened with all his previous convictions. The solicitor will read the forensic report, which will confirm everything the two detectives have said. She'll explain to McLaren that the evidence is overwhelming and that if he continues to plead his innocence but is found guilty by a jury then his sentence will be a lot longer than it would be if he simply pleads guilty now. She will also tell him that she can use the fact that he was drunk when the incident occurred as mitigation and try to reduce the sentence further. She'll suggest that if he's lucky he might even get away with a suspended sentence i.e. no jail time, but will have to do some community service, which is the best he can hope for in the circumstances. He'll suddenly come to his senses and decide to plead guilty in the hope that the Procurator Fiscal will grab the offer with both hands in order to keep their huge workload to a minimum.

The two detectives returned to their office content that this one was in the bag, providing the young solicitor was worth her salt and did her job. Detective Constable Jim Armstrong was first to speak when they entered the room. "Well, did you get a confession?"

"Not yet, Jim," replied DS O'Neill. "But it won't be long. Just letting him and his solicitor stew a bit. Do you want a coffee boss?" he said turning to DI Redding.

"Thanks Brian, but can I have a tea instead please?"

"No problem, I'll put the kettle on."

At that moment, DCI Miller came into the room looking for Claire.

"A young woman has been found dead on the shore at the Bowling Basin. Looks like accidental death by drowning according to the uniforms on site but can you and Brian meet me down there right away Claire?" she said and started to walk out the room.

"Yes Ma'am, but we're in the middle of an interview with McLaren and his solicitor and were just about to go back in and finish off."

The DCI hesitated for a moment as she considered the situation. "Brian can finish the interview and you can meet me down there. Bring Jim instead."

"No problem. See you there in a few minutes," she said, and immediately went for her coat. She turned to Brian who was looking a little deflated. "Sorry Brian. Anyway, you heard the DCI, it might just be an accidental drowning. Nothing to get excited about."

"More likely to be another jumper. It won't be the first time someone has jumped off the Erskine Bridge and their body found further along the river when the tide goes out," said Jim.

"The thought had occurred to me but let's not jump to any conclusions," said Claire putting on her coat and smiling at her own little pun. She knew it would be cold down by the waterside. It didn't matter what time of year it was, but in February it would be absolutely freezing. "Come on Jim, let's go. We don't want to keep the new DCI waiting do we?"

Detective Chief Inspector Patricia Miller had only joined "L" Division in Dumbarton a few months earlier and was very keen to make her mark. Claire had hoped that having a female DCI in charge would be easier to deal with than her previous boss, DCI Thomson, but that was proving not to be the case. The new DCI was every bit as impatient and grumpy as her predecessor and, if anything, appeared to have a grudge against other female officers which Claire couldn't quite understand. It wasn't easy being a woman in the chauvinistic world of policing in Scotland and even harder to be noticed but Claire had made a good start to her career. First, there was her involvement in a major drugs bust in Glasgow and then she had led the CID team in Dumbarton which had solved a series of burglaries and two brutal murders. The latter had been a particularly dangerous and almost fatal for the young detective who would most certainly have been the third victim of the killer had it not been for the timely intervention of her boyfriend, Peter Macdonald. Sadly, one of her team, DC Joseph Docherty, was not so lucky and was killed just before Claire had managed to solve the case. This was something which played on her mind from time to time but now it was even more to the forefront of her thoughts as she and DC Docherty's replacement, DC Jim Armstrong, made their way down to Bowling Basin. The last time she had gone there she had been locked in the boot of a car and was very lucky to have survived the journey. This time was different though and she was keen to make a good impression on the new DCI.

Claire could see the flashing blue lights of a squad car down by the waterfront. "Turn right and follow the road over the bridge and go down to the arches, Jim. We can park down there and walk the rest of the way."

Jim did as he was told and parked his car just outside the wee cycle repair shop. They got out of the car and approached the area where the body had been found, Claire could see that the tide was fully out and the basin had drained completely. The DCI was speaking to one of the police officers on site and from her hand movements, Claire could tell that the DCI was giving out directions on how to secure the area.

"Ah, good you're here Claire," said the DCI. "Take a quick look at the body and tell me what you think?" The DCI pointed down the bank to where the dishevelled body of the young woman was lying like a discarded rag doll; her legs and arms splayed out in a very unnatural position.

Claire nodded and made her way carefully down the slippery bank to get a closer look at the young woman. She could tell from the pale blue colour of the skin that she had been dead for a while. There didn't appear to be any sign of a trauma or bruising to the face, arms or legs, which were all visible, so drowning was a possible cause of death. They would only know for sure once the pathologist had carried out a full autopsy on the body. Claire put on a pair of rubber gloves and knelt down beside the body. She carefully searched the pockets of the jacket the deceased young woman was wearing to see if she was carrying any form of identification but there was nothing. There was also no sign of any jewellery on the body. Claire noticed that the dead woman was quite small, extremely thin, had medium length brown hair, albeit filthy and thick with muck but more significantly was wearing a party dress.

Not something you would choose to wear if you were planning to jump off a bridge, thought Claire.

Claire also noticed that her shoes were missing but they could have fallen off in the water or were kicked off before she jumped. However, what really stuck out was the deceased's finger nails which were completely worn down, some were broken and were extremely dirty.

Having made her initial assessment, Claire climbed back up the steep bank and approached the DCI, who was now in deep conversation with DC Armstrong. "Well Claire, what's your opinion?"

"I'm not sure about the cause of death but I don't think it was suicide. If you consider how she is dressed and the condition of her finger nails, it doesn't really add up."

"I agree, so let's get a forensic team down here as soon as possible. The pathologist is already on his way. Claire, you're the SIO. Once you've finished here, we can discuss how to take the investigation forward. First things first, we need the pathologist to establish cause of death and we need to try and identify the body."

"Will do, Ma'am," said Claire. She was delighted that she had been made Senior Investigation Officer for this one; the DCI could easily have taken control of the case herself.

The pathologist, Richard McAlpine, arrived shortly after the DCI had left the scene. The uniformed police officers in attendance had secured a large perimeter around the area with the usual blue and white police tape and were now patrolling the area to prevent interested onlookers getting anywhere near the scene. Not that there would be anyone around at this time of year but once the local press got a hold of the story they were sure to appear magically like rabbits out of a hat. McAlpine showed his ID to one of the police officers, ducked under the plastic tape and approached DI Redding, who was now speaking to the dog walker who had found the body and had alerted the Police.

"Thank you for your help Mr Baxter. I'll send a police officer around to your home to take a full statement but in the meantime please do not speak to anyone about this, especially the local press."

Mr Baxter nodded in agreement and headed back towards his home with his wee Highland Terrier, which had clearly picked up the scent of the dead body and was desperate to investigate. After a few tugs of the lead and a good telling off, the wee dog finally succumbed to its master's instructions and toddled off, wagging its little pointed tail as it went.

"Is that who found the body?" asked McAlpine, as he approached DI Redding pointing to Mr Baxter.

"Yes, apparently he often walks his dog by the riverside. He says he didn't touch anything and just called the Police as soon as he saw her lying there." She gestured towards the girl's body. "The SOC team is on the way but it would be really good if you could advise on the cause and time of death."

McAlpine, who was at least six feet tall, looked down at the young petite detective with a look of dismay. "It's unlikely that I'll be able to determine time of death here with any form of accuracy given that the body has been in cold water for what looks like some considerable time. And unless the cause of death is obvious, and by that I mean there's a bullet wound to the head or stab wounds to be found on the torso, then I have little chance of identifying the cause of death. I assume if the cause of death was that obvious you would have already told me what you had found in your initial examination of the body. Am I correct?"

Di Redding frowned at the derogatory tone of the pathologist's comments but held back and ignored his little dig at her. "Yes, there's nothing obvious but I did notice the girl's finger nails were damaged and dirty, which was unusual given that she's wearing a party dress. Obviously, the first thought that springs to mind is that she jumped from the bridge and washed up here but who dresses up to commit suicide?"

"Okay, I'll take a good look, measure body temperature, etc., and see what information I can share before I do the full autopsy."

McAlpine made his way carefully down the grassy bank but lost his footing and fell on his backside. Claire burst out laughing but stopped when McAlpine looked up at her, giving her the dirtiest look possible. *Serves you right*, she thought. McAlpine stood up and wiped himself down. He cleaned his dirty hands on his jacket as best he could and then took out a pair of clean surgical gloves and carefully pulled them on, one by one.

Claire watched him as he examined the body, inspected the finger nails and then felt the feet and legs, looking for signs of breaks, possible damage caused if a jumper hit the water feet first. McAlpine finished by taking the body temperature and then recorded the temperature of the river water. When he finished he climbed back up the bank to the young detective.

"There's no sign of any damage to legs or feet. I'll need to get her back to the lab to check if she drowned or not. There's usually some frothing around the mouth with drowning but it could have been washed away. She's certainly been in the water for over 24 hours given her low body temperature but I'll be able to tell you much more once…"

"You get her back to the lab," said Claire anticipating his response.

"Yes, do you want to attend the autopsy?" he asked.

Di Redding was taken aback. She hadn't attended an autopsy before and wasn't sure how she would react. McAlpine could see her hesitancy and smiled.

"You don't need to be there of course, but it will mean that you won't have to wait for my report if I discover anything significant that could assist with your enquiries."

"Yes, makes sense. Let me know when you have scheduled it and I'll be there."

"Great, it'll be later this afternoon providing the forensics team don't take all day doing their bit. I'll get my office to call you and confirm the time. Don't be late as I won't wait for you," he said and walked away briskly.

"Yes sir," she said under her breath sarcastically and saluted him behind his back. *What an arse!,* she thought to herself.

DI Redding stayed at the scene until the SOC team arrived. After giving them detailed instructions, she called DS O'Neill and asked him to set up the incident room. Their priority now was to identify body and find out as a much as possible about the dead girl. Brian confirmed that the DCI had already briefed him and that DC Jackson was currently searching missing persons for a match with the dead girl. Satisfied that everything was being done that could be done, she decided to head back to the station to take charge of the team.

Chapter Four

The Council Offices in Dumbarton were now proudly located in the centre of the town. The state of the art award winning building was cleverly built behind the façade of the Old Academy Buildings, which had lain derelict for many years and had become an eye sore.

Behind its traditional yellow sandstone façade was a suite of very modern offices plus the new Civic Space which hosted the meetings of the Council and its committees along with other large civic events. The Council Offices in Dumbarton had previously been located at Garshake Road next to the Police headquarters but time had taken its toll on the dilapidated concrete building and the decision had been taken to build a new more eco-efficient building in the Town Centre. It was also hoped that the new building and all the Council staff who worked there would rejuvenate the town centre but all that had really been achieved was a growth in cafés and snack shops which appear to be thriving due to the additional lunchtime footfall.

The cavernous Civic Space was located at the front of the building with the original window arches of the Old Academy building allowing natural light to fill the unique room. With its strange mix of modern furniture and equipment, balanced by some historical paintings depicting some of the most rich and famous sons and daughters of Dumbarton, not to mention a huge painting of Queen Victoria arriving on the Royal Yacht at Dumbarton Castle, this was indeed an appropriate location for the seat of local government in West Dunbartonshire.

At precisely 10 am, the Convener of the Planning Committee, Councillor Jack Caldwell, called the meeting to commence and quickly moved through the standing items on the agenda until reaching the first and most controversial application of the day – a proposal to build a new supermarket on the grounds of the former site of Ballantyne's brewery, which once was one of the largest employers in the town but had since closed leaving its large red brick building and iconic towers on the shore of the Clyde derelict and neglected. Dumbarton already had two large supermarkets which had been widely blamed for destroying the town centre and now planning officers were controversially recommending that permission be granted to allow another one to be built on a prime site facing the river.

After briefly hearing the senior planning officer outline the terms of the application and explain the reasons for recommending approval subject to a number of strict conditions in terms of design of the new supermarket and its surrounding grounds and car park, the Convener invited the first objector, Councillor Taylor to speak for no more than five minutes, as was specified in the procedure. Councillor John Taylor, who represented the Dumbarton Ward, was a staunch objector to the proposal, was permitted to speak out publicly against the application as he was not a member of the Planning Committee. Any member of the Planning Committee who did this would automatically exclude themselves from the decision making process.

"Thank you, Chair. I speak today on behalf of over 200 local people from within my Ward who are outraged at the prospect of yet another supermarket being built in the heart of Dumbarton. Our objections are not just based on planning considerations but also in terms of the economic impact that another supermarket would have on our beleaguered town centre." He paused a little thus allowing the rapturous applause from the public gallery to subside before continuing. "Members of the Planning Committee, may I remind you that it was not so very long ago when this Committee met up in Garshake Road and decided to move these very offices to the town centre and why? To rejuvenate the town centre which was once the very heart and soul of this proud town. This proposal will destroy everything we have done to date as more small business fail to compete with the greedy supermarket giants and we will be left with nothing but charity shops, public houses, chemists and banks in our High Street and now even the banks are starting to close. Now, I know that the Planning Committee is not allowed to consider such economic matters directly but as I mentioned before there are also strong planning considerations which must be taken into account. First of all, we have a fantastic opportunity, nay an unique opportunity, to build something wonderful on the banks of the River Clyde which we can all be proud of and will attract tourists and generate revenue for local businesses in this area. I'm afraid, building another pig ugly supermarket and car park on the waterfront will do none of these things. I appreciate the planning officer has insisted on a number of environmental conditions being attached to the application but these do not go far enough and quite frankly are nothing more than window dressing. A few trees here, a few shrubs there, will not disguise this hideous carbuncle of a building. I ask the Committee to listen to the local people and vote against this dreadful application. Thank you, Chair."

The public gallery exploded into applause at the end of the speech and the Convener tried his best to calm them down before inviting the next objector to speak. Among the other objectors in the public gallery, was a well known local business man, Donald Gallagher, who was also a staunch supporter of everything historic in Dumbarton, in particular, Dumbarton Castle, of which he was a custodian. After everyone had been heard, the Committee debated the application at length. It was clear that some of the Members on the Committee supported the view that the new supermarket would bring more jobs to the area and therefore were of the opinion that subject to the conditions suggested by the planning officer being agreed, the supermarket would be an asset to the town and would create jobs in the long term. However, after a lengthy and sometimes heated debate, the majority voted against the application to the pleasure of the public gallery.

After the meeting was over Donald Gallagher waited for Councillor Taylor outside the council chamber.

"Well done Councillor, I could not have done it better myself."

"Thanks Donald, but it's not over yet. I understand the applicant intends to appeal to the Scottish Government."

"Ach, you'll see that lot off as well. Let's go for a pint and celebrate today's victory."

"Sorry, I wish I could but I have an appeal hearing this afternoon in Clydebank so I need to go home and prepare for that."

Donald let out a small sigh. "Ah well, a councillor's work is never done I suppose! Okay, we can get together when you're less busy and I can update you on the work up at the castle."

"That would be great. I'll be in touch, bye for now." Councillor Taylor headed to his car which was in the main car park at the rear of the building. Donald Gallagher went in the opposite direction towards his van which was parked behind the Masonic Halls. He had a skip in his step and whistled all the way back to his vehicle.

Chapter Five

DI Redding was standing in a corner of the room wearing a blue gown and face mask. The body of the dead girl was lying on a cold stainless steel table, completely naked and void of all dignity. The first thing which struck the DI was that the girl was extremely thin. Claire shivered at the thought of what was about to happen and wasn't entirely sure how she would react when McAlpine started making his cuts.

McAlpine was standing over the body, dictating notes which were being recorded from an overhead microphone immediately above him. He started by describing the overall condition of the girl's body; her skin tone, hair colour, eye colour, height and more significantly her weight. He went on to comment on every mark or abrasion he could see on the body and paid particular attention to the finger nails. He scraped some of the dirt from under the finger nails of both hands and placed the samples carefully into a small plastic bag which he passed to his assistant to label and record.

He then examined her groin area and then took some swabs from the outside and inside of the vaginal area. "No obvious sign of rape or sexual activity," he said for the benefit of the recording. He turned to face DI Redding. "There's no torn tissue or sign of bleeding or indeed any sign of semen."

His first incision was from top to bottom of the breast plate. Having peeled away the skin, he then cut open the rib cage and removed the lungs one at a time. His assistant weighed each lung and then McAlpine carefully dissected a small section of one of the lungs and examined the spongy tissue which he squeezed gently between two fingers, carefully examining the content. He turned towards DI Redding. "There's no obvious sign of drowning either; there's no frothing in the airways or any sign of sea water or other debris in the lungs, which would be expected if salt water had been inhaled. I'll send samples of the lung tissue off for further chemical analysis but my gut feeling at the moment is that she was dead before she entered the water."

"So what was the cause of death?" asked DI Redding.

"I'm not sure yet," he said and promptly went back to examining the body. He went on to remove the heart, kidneys, stomach and liver from the body and passed to his assistant to weigh each organ. The assistant read aloud the weight for the purpose of the recording and McAlpine then took the stomach and cut it open on a separate tray. At this point, DI Redding felt her own stomach leap and threw up in the small plastic bin that McAlpine had kindly offered to her at the start of the examination. He knew she would need it at some point.

McAlpine waited for the young detective to recover and compose herself before speaking. "Well I can't be sure of cause of death but it appears that she certainly suffered from starvation before she died." He went on to explain in more detail.

"When the body uses its reserves to provide basic energy needs, it can no longer supply the necessary nutrients to vital organs and tissues. The heart, lungs, and even the ovaries shrink. All the organs I have removed so far suggest that this is the case; they are far smaller than you would expect to find in a healthy female adult. In addition, her stomach was not only smaller than one would expect but it was completely empty, which is also unusual. Did you notice how pale her skin was?"

"Yes, but I put that down to her being in the water for so long."

McAlpine nodded. "I did at first as well but look at her hands. Normally you would see a difference in the colour of hands and arms at the wrists where clothing stops sunlight reaching the lower arm. In this case there is almost no difference at all. My guess is that she has not had much access to sunlight over a prolonged period."

DI Redding considered this new information. "So what you are suggesting is that she was locked away somewhere with no natural light and then was starved to death? Oh my God, the poor girl!"

"That's my gut feeling at the moment. I'll need to take further samples which will either confirm or dismiss my theory. For example, we'll be able to tell from the bone tissue if she lacks Vitamin D or not. As you probably know, Vitamin D is produced when the skin is exposed to sunlight. Therefore, we will be able to check for this as well as other signs of light starvation, such as rickets and weakened bones."

"So, it looks like she has been locked away for some time, possible cause of death is starvation …and her finger nails? Damaged while trying to escape or scrape her way out of the locked room, perhaps?" suggested DI Redding.

"That would be my best guess for now but I'll continue to do further tests and let you know when the results come back from the lab. Oh, and I'll send samples of the dirt that I removed from under the nails to the lab to see if they can identify a possible location based on the chemical analysis of the dirt. You never know what that can reveal."

"Elementary, my dear Watson?" she said.

"What?"

"Sorry, it's one of Sherlock Holmes famous sayings. Apparently, soil analysis was only introduced as a method of detection after Conan Doyle had published some of his earlier Sherlock Holmes novels. Of course, Holmes did all his own research and analysis; he didn't have the luxury of a full lab of technicians available to help him."

"You are aware that it was all a work of fiction?" said McAlpine smiling.

"Ha ha, you're such a funny guy!" she said. "But, seriously, the scientific methods described in Arthur Conan Doyle's books have assisted with criminal investigation ever since. Anyway, thank you for allowing me to be here. There's now no doubt in my mind that there is enough evidence to suggest that the circumstances around this death are at the very least suspicious and require further investigation."

"You're welcome. I'll send you the full report as soon as possible."

DI Redding left the room and headed back to the station. She was keen to share this new information with the DCI and the rest of the team but also eager to know if Brian had any luck identifying the girl. She dreaded the thought of the conversation she would need to have with the poor girl's parents.

Chapter Six

George Duncan was sitting in his living room speaking to Detective Sergeant Andy Bell from the CID team in Maryhill. Detective Constable Alice McWilliams was sitting in the opposite corner of the room taking notes as Mr Duncan responded to her colleague's questions. Unlike the experienced and battle worn DS Bell, Alice McWilliams was new to the job and was still full of enthusiasm and excitement. She had always wanted to be a detective and now had the chance to shine in her new role.

Catherine Duncan had gone to bed with a migraine caused by stress. She had taken a couple of strong pain killers and had finally fallen asleep just before the two detectives had arrived. George didn't have the heart to wake her up and so had decided to conduct this particular interview on his own.

DS Bell slowly went through all the information previously covered in the statement taken by PC Downie earlier in the day and was now convinced that neither of Anne's parents had anything to do with her disappearance. "Can you think of anyone who would want to hurt Anne, Mr Duncan? An old boyfriend, a jealous friend or colleague from work?"

"No, I'm sorry, I really can't think of anyone."

"Okay, thank you, but if you think of anything please do not hesitate to call my number," he said and handed over a small business card to Mr Duncan who promptly looked at it and placed it on the mantelpiece.

"So, what happens next?"

"Just so you are aware, we have managed to get copies of CCTV footage from inside the public house where Anne was drinking with her friends. We're also looking at CCTV taken from street cameras in Argyll Street and hopefully that might help us find out who..." he stopped speaking as Mrs Duncan entered the room.

"Oh hello love, this is Detective Sergeant Bell and Detective Constable McWilliams. They were just explaining what will happen next."

Cathy sat down beside George on the settee. Her head was still a bit groggy from the painkillers but at least the migraine had lifted. She acknowledged the two detectives but wasn't really listening to what her husband was saying.

"Have you heard anything? Has there been any news?" she asked.

"No, I'm sorry Mrs Duncan. Nothing so far but I was just explaining to your husband that we have managed to get CCTV footage from inside the pub where Anne was drinking. We also have identified some of the street cameras in Argyll Street, near the bus stop where she normally got the bus home, so hopefully we will find something which might help explain what has happened to your daughter. As you know we have already circulated a photograph of your daughter to all local police stations in and around Glasgow and have now put an appeal out to local press and on social media seeking any information on what might have happened to Anne. You might see it reported on Reporting Scotland tonight or hear it on the radio so just be prepared for..."

"Will we need to appear on telly? I've seen others do that?" asked Cathy.

"Only, if you want to," replied DC McWilliams. "We wouldn't ask you to do anything which makes you feel uncomfortable or upsets you."

Cathy just sat there, nodded and then started to weep.

"We'll have a think about it," said George putting his arm around Cathy to comfort her.

"No problem, we'll leave you both in peace for now and will be in touch if there are any developments."

The two officers made their way back to the police car.

"Well, what do you think?" asked DS Bell.

"It's all a bit of a mystery. I don't think either of them was involved, do you?"

"Not a chance. Let's get back to the station and see what the CCTV footage reveals."

Chapter Seven

As Claire entered the CID Office, she could sense there was a real buzz of excitement about the place. It had been a while since her team had been given a murder to investigate and she could see that the case had given them a new source of motivation and energy, which had been sadly lacking in recent weeks. DS O'Neill was the first to notice the DI arrive and immediately got to his feet.

"I think we've identified her, boss," he said waving a photo of a girl in his hands. Claire took the photo of the girl and read the details printed at the foot of the page.

"Lisa Chandler, 360 East Street, Helensburgh. She went missing …8 months ago! Oh my God, the poor girl."

"What did the autopsy reveal? Anything conclusive?" asked Brian.

"Yes, it looks like she starved to death."

"You're kidding, she actually starved to death?" he said rubbing his head in disbelief. He couldn't go beyond lunchtime without a roll and sausage and a cup of tea.

Claire could read his mind but continued without comment.   "I also think that she was held in captivity until she died, that is before her body was dumped in the Clyde. McAlpine has taken various samples of body tissue for further analysis to try to confirm the cause of death. Oh, and soil was taken from her fingernails and sent to the forensics lab to see if we can get some idea as to where she was being held.   So, for now, we treat this as a suspicious death. I'll go and tell the Chief and then we'll need to go and tell the girl's parents and ask them to identify the body.   Until we have the positive ID, all we tell the parents is that a body was found in the river which matches the description of their daughter. Understood?"

The look on Brian's face gave away how he was feeling about the last part. "Yes boss, I hate this bit of the job."

"Me too, but it needs to be done. Once we have a positive ID we can find out more about the circumstances leading up to the girl's disappearance. Can you pull the file while I brief the DCI?"

Brian nodded in compliance and immediately went to his pc to access the missing person's file. He quickly found what he was looking for and printed two copies of the report; one for him and one for the DI.

Chapter Eight

The dark grey unmarked squad car turned right off the A814 at the County Hotel and then turned left into South King Street, passing the small community fire station on the left.

DI Redding looked admiringly at the neat row of semi-detached bungalows with their white walls and their red Mediterranean style tiled roofs and tidy little gardens and driveways to the front. The houses reminded her of the street where her parents lived; full of middle class people who spent their weekends washing their cars and tending to their gardens. It was so very different from the life she had chosen for herself, and was also very different from the life her parents would have chosen for their beloved daughter. They had grand plans for Claire who had graduated from Glasgow University with a first class honours degree in mathematics. They thought she would be a teacher or an accountant but she was having none of that and as it turned out her analytical brain was very suited to solving crime and she loved it. All her life she had loved solving puzzles and nothing gave her greater satisfaction than solving crimes.

The car turned left at the end of the road and entered East King Street.

"What was the house number again?" asked Brian looking around, trying to read the house numbers as he drove.

Some of the properties had the numbers on the outside walls while others only had them beside the front door and therefore were difficult to read from the road.

Claire quickly looked down at the file. "It's 360, even numbers are on your right."

They counted down the numbers until they found the Chandler's house and pulled in just beyond the black iron gates to the property, which were lying opened. Claire got out the car first and headed down the small gravel driveway leading to the front door and rang the bell. She noticed that there was a small light blue Beetle parked to the side of house so she was hopeful that someone was home.

The impressive red wooden door of the house was opened by a small middle aged woman. She had blonde greying hair and was wearing grey dungarees, a blue cardigan over a plain white t-shirt and was holding a pair of secateurs in her hand. "Sorry to keep you, I was out in the garden. Can I help you?"

"Hello, I'm Detective Inspector Claire Redding and this is my colleague, Detective Sergeant Brian O'Neill." Both officers produced their warrant cards and presented them to Mrs Chandler.

"Are you Mrs Elizabeth Chandler?" asked Claire.

"Yes, is this about Lisa?" she asked, eagerly awaiting a response.

"Can we come in Mrs Chandler?" asked Claire looking over the small woman's shoulder towards the inside of the house.

"What, yes, of course." She led the two police officers into a large living room which was filled with two rather old matching leather sofas and a leather lounge chair, which had also seen better days.

"Well, have you found Lisa?" she asked again, this time with a little more anxiety in her voice.

"Please sit down, Mrs Chandler," said DI Redding. The young detective took a deep breath before breaking the bad news. "The body of a girl matching Lisa's description has been found in the River Clyde." DI Redding paused while the shock of this news sunk in. "However, we will need to ask you or your husband to identify the body before we can be one hundred percent sure that it's her. Where is Mr Chandler at the moment?"

Mrs Chandler started to weep. "He'll be on his way back from work. How did she die, was she drowned, what happened?"

"I'm afraid we can't reveal any information about the cause of death until we get a positive identification of the body."

"So, it might not be our Lisa then? You said can't be sure so you need me to identify the body, right?" she asked, looking firstly at DI Redding and then to DS O'Neill praying that one of them would give her a glimmer of hope.

This time DS O'Neill chose to respond. "Mrs Chandler, we believe the girl who was found earlier today is Lisa but we need confirmation. I'm so sorry Mrs Chandler but…"

The conversation was interrupted by the sound of a car pulling into the driveway and Mrs Chandler immediately got up and looked out of the large bay window to see who it was.

"That's Keith now." She went to the door to greet her husband and share the news but all she could do when he came in was cry while hugging him as tightly as she could. Keith Chandler dropped his bag by the door. "What's going on? What's the matter, Betty?"

"The police are here. They think they have found Lisa. She's dead Keith, they found her body in the Clyde," she blurted out between sobs.

"What? What do you mean?" he said suddenly taken aback with shock. He gently pushed his wife away and entered the living room. "What's going on?" he demanded.

Claire stood up and introduced herself. She quickly explained what had happened and eventually managed to calm him down. After he had composed himself he agreed that he would go to the mortuary to identify the body as he didn't think Betty would cope very well. Initially, she argued with him and insisted that they both should go but finally agreed that it would be for the best.

Chapter Nine

Robert was sitting watching the two small monitors which were fed from the two tiny spy cameras which he had installed in each corner of the cell. It was amazing what you could buy on the internet these days. The two cameras were well hidden and high enough out of reach to be accidentally or deliberately damaged. One of the cameras was infrared and could show images even when the room was in complete darkness. However, as the light was currently on in the room the image coming from the infrared camera was blurred and consequently his attention was on the other screen.

He sat there for hours taking copious notes on Anne's behaviour as this element of the analysis was just as important to his research as were the conversations which he had recorded using a hidden microphone in the light switch. He was really pleased with how well the first conversation had gone and was hopeful that *this time* his experiment would be more productive. Indeed he was so pleased with Anne's performance that he had made a meal for her even though she had broken the no swearing rule. The fact that she refused to eat it was neither here nor there as she would soon give in to her hunger. He was sure of that.

After a few hours of observation, it was now obvious from the low snoring sound coming from the room that Anne had managed to fall asleep and so he decided to take a break and get something to eat. He made his way to the exit and could smell the sea air rush into the dark corridor as he opened the door and climbed up towards the large drain cover which served as the secret entrance to his den. He could hear the gulls calling in the distance as he made his way down towards the Governor's House when suddenly he heard a voice, calling over to him.

"Hey, what are you doing here? You shouldn't be here!"

Shit! He had been seen.

Chapter Ten

Peter Macdonald was busy cooking a meal for himself and Claire. As usual Sally, his black and white Cocker Spaniel, was lying in her bed in the corner of the room watching Peter as he prepared the food. She had already been fed but was hoping that some scraps would be forthcoming when Peter and Claire were finished eating.

Peter heard the front door open and Sally immediately jumped to her feet to go and greet Claire as she entered the room. "Hello," she said as she entered the kitchen. "What's all this, candles, best cutlery and what's that you're cooking - steaks? What's the occasion?"

Peter turned around with a huge grin on his face. "Don't you remember?"

Her face went blank.

"Today is the first anniversary of the day that you moved in."

"Is it really?" she asked genuinely surprised at how quickly the time had passed.

"Yes, I knew you wouldn't remember but that's fine because I wanted it to be a surprise. SURPRISE!"

"Sorry, I'm hopeless with dates. Oh, but this is lovely, Peter. Have I got time to go upstairs and get changed before we eat?"

"You've got five minutes. I've just put the steaks on and wouldn't want them to over cook."

Claire walked over to him and gave him a huge hug. "You're the best, Peter Macdonald. You really are!" She kissed him on the cheek and headed off to get ready as Peter kept a watchful eye on the steaks. He was really pleased that Claire was in a good mood and he was very excited at the thought of what he was about to ask her. He had been waiting for the right moment for some time now and had selected an engagement ring which he was sure Claire would love. It was a bit of a risk as they hadn't really talked about marriage but he was confident that she would say yes as their relationship was really strong, their love making was great and they had been living together for just over a year now so why not tie the knot! He could feel the small ring box in his pocket pressing against his leg and decided to hide it in a kitchen drawer as Claire might notice the small bulge in his pocket. She missed nothing! He thought back to their first meeting and smiled to himself. Sally had escaped his grip on the way to the vets and ran straight into Claire who was coming out of Asda with bags of shopping in her hands. She ended up on her knees with crushed shopping bags but had got up without any fuss. He loved that about her. He also thought back to the first time she had come to his home and how worried she had been to tell him that she was a police officer. As if that would have put him off! He was head over heels in love with her and she had told him that she loved him. *Life couldn't get any better than this.*

Claire came skipping down the stairs. She was wearing a maroon dress which complemented the shape of her petite figure. She was gorgeous. Peter was pleased that she had made the effort to get dressed up and began to wonder if she had guessed what he had planned. He quickly served up the meal and opened a bottle of their favourite red wine. "Here's to us," he said, and raised his glass.

They quickly devoured what had come to be one of their favourite meals: fillet steak, French fries, fried onions, mushrooms and cooked tomatoes on the vine. Peter stood up to clear the plates away and went to get the ring as now was the perfect time to pop the question and then …the house phone rang.

"I'll get it," said Claire before he could stop her. "Hello, oh hi Mum, how are you? What? When? Oh God! Do you know who is dealing with the case? Yes, of course. No, leave it with me and I'll find out what I can." Claire hung up the phone. Her face was ashen and Peter could tell something bad had happened.

"What's the matter Claire?" he asked, hoping desperately that she had over reacted but deep down he knew that he was going to regret asking.

"That was my Mum, she says that Anne Duncan has gone missing!"

"Who's Anne Duncan?" asked Peter.

"She's my wee cousin."

Chapter Eleven

DC Alice McWilliams was sitting at her desk looking at the CCTV footage that had been taken from one of the street cameras which pointed to the area near the bus stop where Anne Duncan had been taken. By sheer good luck the camera had captured the whole abduction from start to finish and this was at least the tenth time the young detective had reviewed the same piece of footage but so far she had not discovered anything knew.

The video images on the screen showed a white unmarked van stopping at the bus stop where Anne Duncan was standing waiting for the bus. A man wearing dark clothing and what appeared to be a black golf cap with a large skip got out of the vehicle and approached Anne who was beginning to look a bit distressed and unsteady on her feet. From a distance it looked like he was helping her;

firstly, taking her arm and putting it over his shoulder for support and then putting his arm around her while walking her carefully to the vehicle. Unfortunately, the camera was positioned at too high an angle to capture any of his face; the golf cap with the large skip had put paid to that and he seemed to know exactly how to avoid the camera by keeping his head down at all times when in direct line of sight. All she could make out from the footage was that he was approximately 5ft 8 inches tall and was of stocky build.

It occurred to Alice that the scene would have appeared very innocent to any onlooker. It would be natural to assume that he was helping the girl, who perhaps had one too many drinks and was worse for wear. *Maybe, that's why no one had come forward with any information so far,* she thought.

The CCTV camera had managed to pick up the registration number of the small van as it headed off towards the expressway but now that they knew its registration number, they could try to trace its path through Glasgow by checking other cameras within the area. A number of police officers were working on this part of the investigation under the watchful eye of DS Bell. They had checked the plates of the van on the DVLA database but they were false, *of course*, and apparently belonged to a similar type vehicle. DC William's concentration was interrupted by a phone ringing from the other side of the room. She looked up to see which phone had a flashing red light on its front panel.

"Andy, I think that's your phone," she shouted across the room.

DS Bell cursed under his breath and went over to his desk. "Hello, DS Bell, Maryhill CID, can I help you? Oh hello Claire...of course I remember you, you were on that big drugs bust here, before heading off to...where? Ah yes, that's right, Dumbarton, as the new DI. What can I do you for?" He paused while DI Redding explained that the missing girl was her cousin and that she was keen to find out how the case was progressing. Did they have any leads? Was there anything she could do to help?

DS Bell outlined very briefly what they had discovered to date and explained that they were currently trying to follow where the van was heading by using the CCTV trail. He promised to keep her up to date but needed to get back to co-ordinating the search for the van as that was all they had to go on at the moment. Claire thanked him for his time and suggested that she might pay him a visit, if that was okay with DS Bell. He reluctantly agreed as a professional courtesy but was slightly concerned given her close relationship to the missing girl. He ended the call by telling her that he would need to check with his superiors and would get back to confirm. She thanked him for his help and ended the call.

DC McWilliams decided she had seen enough of the abduction scene and decided to take another look at the footage captured by CCTV inside the night club. The camera had been positioned above the bar area so didn't cover the full room. However, it did capture Anne and her friends approaching the bar to order some drinks when they first entered the club. The photo that Jean McArthur had provided had been extremely helpful as Anne was easily recognisable even though the lighting in the club was low. Alice watched as people came and went from the bar. It was only after her third viewing that she noticed the outline of a man who had a similar size and build to the van driver. He was standing in the far corner of the bar with his back to the camera. Unfortunately, there was insufficient light to make out any detail but she was able to see that he wasn't wearing a cap and had a full head of dark hair. "Andy, come and have a look at this?"

DS Bell made his way over to her desk and leaned towards the screen.

"So what am I looking at?" he said trying to spot something obvious but failing miserably.

"I've just been looking at the abduction footage again and then went back to the CCTV in the club. Look over here, it's very dark but I'm convinced this is the same man who was driving the van."

He looked closely at the image and then agreed. "Well spotted! Okay let's try and get a better copy of the image. See if the technical team can lighten it up a bit. Then we should interview all the bar staff on duty that night and see if anyone recognises him."

"Will do," said Alice. "Who was on the phone?"

"Eh, oh yeah, that was DI Claire Redding from Dumbarton CID. Apparently she's related to Anne

Duncan and wanted to know how we were getting on with the investigation. She offered to help given that she knows Anne really well."

"Is that allowed?"

"I'll need to check with the DCI, but I seriously doubt it. She's emotionally involved in the case and that is never a good thing. Although, if it were my relative I'd want to know what was happening. Don't get me wrong; I'm happy to keep her informed, of course, but at a distance, if you know what I mean. Anyhow, it'll be the DCI's call."

Chapter Twelve

DI Redding and DS O'Neill had agreed to meet with Keith Chandler at the mortuary at 10 am. The two police officers arrived just before 10 am and entered the building where both Mr and Mrs Chandler were waiting. Claire approached the nervous couple who sat together in silence just holding each others hand for support.

"Hello, I see you've both decided to come. Do you both want to identify the body?" asked Claire, being careful not to make any assumptions but also giving Mrs Chandler the final opportunity to change her mind.

Keith Chandler started to speak but was cut off by his wife. "Yes, I just felt I had to be here, to be sure that the girl was our Lisa."

"Of course, just wait here and I'll make sure we're ready to let you see her."

Claire was gone for a few minutes and when she returned she could see that Brian was briefing the couple as sensitively as he could on the procedure.

"Okay, we're ready for you now," said Claire. "If you would just like to follow me this way please," said Claire.

Claire took them along the narrow corridor and stopped outside a door which led to a small room which had a large square window on its back wall. The couple entered the room, still holding hands which meant they had to squeeze themselves sideways awkwardly through the narrow entrance way. DS Redding and DS O'Neill followed them inside the room. A mortuary assistant saw them arrive and approached the window where the body lay under a cold white sheet. She removed the top of the sheet to reveal the girl's face and almost instantly Mrs Chandler burst into tears. It was clear to Claire and Brian that the girl was Lisa Chandler but nevertheless they had to seek confirmation.

"Mr Chandler. Can you confirm that this is your daughter, Lisa?" asked Brian.

Keith Chandler turned towards DS O'Neill, his eyes full of tears, his lower lip trembling, trying desperately to hold back the emotions which were quickly overpowering his self control. "Yes," he said wiping his eyes. "It's our Lisa." He turned towards the window again just to make sure but there was no doubt. There had never been any doubt. Their last hope that this nightmare was just one big mistake had been completely blown away. This was real, their precious daughter was dead.

"How did she die?" he asked, finally composing himself enough to speak.

His wife was now bent down, almost kneeling on the floor, howling while Claire stood over her, her hand on her shoulder but remaining silent, unable to think of anything to say to the mother who had just lost her child.

"We're not sure yet. The pathologist thinks she may have starved to death and is currently carrying out further tests to confirm that."

"Starved herself to death? How did she end up in the water? That's what you said wasn't it. You found her body in the Clyde?"

Claire looked Mr Chandler face on. "That's correct. We don't know yet how she got into the water but the pathologist has confirmed that she did not drown which means her death is being treated as suspicious." Claire paused and took a deep breath. "And for that reason, we would like to speak to you both. Just to go over the circumstances leading to her disappearance and to gather as much information as possible; to try to understand what happened to Lisa."

Keith Chandler's emotions suddenly leapt from sadness to uncontrollable anger. "What, you think that we had something to do with Lisa's disappearance, her death, is that it?" he shouted.

DS O'Brian stepped forward sensing that Chandler could suddenly become violent. "Mr Chandler, please. We're only trying to find out what happened to your daughter. That's all. When you first reported her missing, the police officer who took the statements was only dealing with a case of a missing person and had no reason to suspect that any harm would or could come to Lisa. However, now that we are investigating a suspicious death we have to be absolutely sure that nothing was missed. Do you understand?"

This appeared to appease Mr Chandler and he slowly nodded back to DS O'Neill.

"Okay, so let's get you both back home safely and we can go over your statements there. I'll drive you in your car and DI Redding will follow in the squad car. We'll also arrange for a police liaison officer to stay with you. The liaison officer will keep you up to date with the investigation and will be there to help if there's any trouble from the media and so on.

Keith Chandler bent down to help his wife get up onto her feet. She had stopped crying and now appeared to have gone completely into herself. She had heard her husband's outburst and the police response but none of that mattered to her. Lisa was gone and nothing that the police investigation would find would help her deal with the deep debilitating pain of the grief that she felt at that moment.

When they got outside the building Claire took Brian aside. "Thanks for that Brian, I thought he was going to tear my head off in there."

"No problem, boss."

"No really, well done! You handled that really well."

"Thanks boss," he said almost blushing. He wasn't used to being complimented and always felt a bit awkward when it happened.

"Now let's get back to their house and try to find out more about how their daughter went missing. Oh and Brian, keep within the speed limit. No blue lights remember," she said pointing to the Chandlers car.

"No, but you have," he said smiling, pointing back to the squad car.

"Only in an emergency Brian, only in an emergency!" she said smiling and headed towards the squad car.

The journey between Glasgow and Helensburgh was fairly uneventful. Brian had opted for the Clyde Expressway and then travelled up through Knightswood and onto the A82. However, instead of connecting to the A814 in Dumbarton he continued on the A82, alongside Loch Lomond, before turning up onto the Blackhill and back down towards the centre of Helensburgh. Brian often argued with his colleagues that this road was quicker due to the higher speed limits on the A82 and so he would take this route instead of going via the low road down by the Clyde. He hadn't noticed that Claire had gone the other way until he arrived at the Chandler's home, where she was standing waiting for him, looking very smug. *Damn,* he thought to himself. *I'll never live this down!* He got out of the car and let Mr and Mrs Chandler lead the way to the house.

Claire followed in behind him quietly humming the tune to that well known Scottish song 'The Bonnie Banks of Loch Lomond'. Although in her head Claire had replaced the reference to 'I'll be in Scotland before ye' to 'I'll be in Helensburgh before ye!'.

It didn't take Brian very long to make the connection. "Very funny," he said turning towards Claire and stuck his tongue out.

Claire just smiled back at her portly colleague and ushered him into the house where Mr and Mrs Chandler were now anxiously waiting for them.

They all sat down in the front room. The Chandlers chose to sit together on the settee beside the large bay window while DI Redding and DS O'Neill sat separately in the other two settees facing the couple. DS O'Neill took out a small note pad and pen from his jacket pocket. He didn't like using the electronic notepads that the uniformed Police now used for recording statements and still preferred to type up his notes back in the office, albeit on a computer and not a typewriter like they had when he first started with the force.

"I'd like to go over your original statements first, if that's okay," said Claire. "We just want to make sure we have all the facts correct and then we'll move onto any other questions that we think might be relevant." Both of the Chandlers just nodded in silence overwhelmed by grief, both utterly despondent. Neither had spoken a word in the car despite Brian's best effort to engage in conversation.

Claire opened the small brown folder that she had been carrying and removed a copy of the original statements. She went over all the information methodically, ensuring that they confirmed all parts of the statement were accurate as she went. They didn't change anything or offer any additional information.

The couple confirmed that Lisa went into Helensburgh to meet a few friends for a meal and some drinks. She had left the house on foot at 8.30 pm on the Saturday night and had never been seen again until her body had washed up on the shores of the Clyde. She hadn't met with her friends who had waited for almost half an hour before calling her parents, who then immediately called the local Police. The Police had taken statements and interviewed all Lisa's friends but they had no clue as to her whereabouts. It was a complete mystery and accordingly Lisa Chandler was added to the long list of missing persons held on file by Police Scotland, who had effectively given up on the search for the missing girl. Police resources were limited and without any clues to go on the officer in charge of the investigation had to make the tough decision to stop actively looking. However, there had been a fair bit of press and media coverage at the time; indeed Lisa's closest friends had put out an alert on Facebook and Twitter but nothing had come back which would help to explain her disappearance. It was now clear to DI Redding that Lisa had been taken that night and held in captivity somewhere until recently but why? That was the real question, the answer to which could unlock the case.

"Thank you both, that was very helpful and I'm sorry I had to put you through that again. I can only imagine how difficult this is for you both. I'm truly sorry. Claire paused for a few seconds while she gathered her thoughts.

"Can you tell us a bit more about Lisa?

"What do you want to know?" asked Mr. Chandler.

"Anything which might help such as where she worked, where she studied, what she did in her spare time, who her friends were?" asked Claire as softly as her voice would allow.

"She was working as a child psychologist for the local education authority; she would help schools deal with children who had difficulties settling in at school or had problems at home, you know the sort of thing."

Claire nodded. "Is that with Argyll and Bute Council or West Dunbartonshire?"

"Argyll and Bute, she had only just started the job when she…she disappeared," he said trying to hold back his emotions as best he could.

"Where did she study? I assume she would need to be qualified?" asked Claire.

"Yes, Glasgow University. She got a First Class Masters degree in Psychology and then went onto complete her PHD in Child Psychology in St Andrews."

"I studied at Glasgow Uni'," said Claire. "Although, my degree was in boring old mathematics; not quite as interesting as psychology."

"Mathematics! What are you doing in the Police with a maths degree?" asked Mrs Chandler, now taking an interest in the conversation.

"Funny enough, that's what my mother thinks. She wanted me to go into teaching," said Claire. Talking about her mother suddenly reminded Claire about the phone call and her cousin Anne's disappearance. She took a mental note to call Maryhill station again when she was finished with the Chandlers. It also occurred to her that Anne had studied at Glasgow University but that was probably just a coincidence, after all thousands of students studied there every year. Claire's mind had wandered only for a few seconds but she suddenly became aware that everyone in the room was staring at her.

"Sorry, I was just gathering my thoughts. So Lisa studied in Glasgow. Did she go out a lot in Glasgow with her friends from Uni'?"

"Sometimes, she did keep in touch with a couple of them but then none of them lived close by so they would meet in Glasgow from time to time. One of them actually tried to get in touch after she disappeared and was really upset when we told her the news."

"Of course, she would be. Do you have her name and contact number? We would like to speak with her about Lisa and find out as much as possible about their time at university."

"I'm sure we have it written down somewhere," said Mrs Chandler who immediately got up and went over to the small sideboard at the back of the room, where they kept the address book.

"Yes, here it is. We agreed to let her know if Lisa came home. I suppose we'll need to let her know that Lisa is dead," she said as tears began to roll down her cheeks again. She wiped her eyes with the sleeve of her top and looked down at the book trying hard to focus her eyes through the mist. "Joyce McLeish, her number is here," she said and read it out aloud.

Brian jotted down the details and thanked Mrs Chandler for the information.

"Can you also provide the contact details for Lisa's other friends; we would like to interview them all, if possible?" asked Claire.

"I'm sure Lisa kept her own address book in her room upstairs, I'll go and get it," said Mrs Chandler. Just as she got up to fetch the book the doorbell rang.

"Who can that be?" asked Mrs Chandler.

Brian stood up and looked out the window. "I think that's the Police Liaison Officer we mentioned earlier. Wait here and I'll get the door."

"Come on in Jenny," said Brian as he opened the door. "We're all in the front room."

PC Jenny Barnes was an experienced liaison officer who had spent 10 years on the beat before deciding that her skills were better served elsewhere in the force. Having tried out a few different roles, she had eventually decided that this line of work suited her. She had also been told by other officers that she was good at it which made all the difference to her. She entered the room behind DS O'Neill who made some brief introductions.

"I'm sorry for your loss, if there's anything I can do to help you though this difficult time, please just ask me," she said looking first at Mrs Chandler and then Mr Chandler. "I'll do my best to keep out your way and give you as much privacy as you need but I'm here to support you."

"Thanks Jenny, said Claire. "We're almost finished here. Just a few more questions and we'll get out of the way. Mrs Chandler was just about to get Lisa's address book and…"

"Oh, yes, I'll get it now," said Mrs Chandler and went off to fetch it.

"Mr Chandler, what did Lisa like to do in her spare time? Any particular hobbies or interests?" asked Claire.

"She was a member of the Helensburgh Tennis Club, oh, and she loved horse riding. There are stables just by Colgrain Farm; she's been going there for years."

"Anything else?" asked Claire.

Betty Chandler came back into the room with a small note book and handed it to DS O'Neill. "I've marked all Lisa's friends that I know of with a yellow highlighter to make it easier for you."

"Thank you, that's very helpful," he replied and flicked through the pages.

"I was just asking your husband if Lisa had any hobbies or interests, Mrs Chandler, said Claire. "He's mentioned tennis and horse riding. Was there anything else?"

"No, I don't think so. Well, she loved going to the cinema but that's not really a hobby, is it?"

"Which cinema did she go to?" asked Claire. "The local one in the old church, I've heard it's pretty good."

"The Tower? Yes, she did go there but I think she preferred going into Glasgow as there was a better choice of movie and the seats were more comfy."

"Yes, I don't fancy sitting on pews for two hours although I do like the settees at the back," said Claire. "Well that's all my questions for now. If you think of anything else which might help please let Jenny know."

Claire couldn't help but think that this case was going to be very difficult. They had very little to go on, no witnesses or CCTV. She could only hope that the lab was able to find something from the samples taken from Lisa's finger nails.

Claire and Brian left the house and headed back to Dumbarton via the low road. Claire had decided to call the team together to do a full update on what they had learned so far and work out what to do next.

Chapter Thirteen

Claire had gathered her team in the incident room and was about to start the briefing when the DCI came into the room.

"Hello Ma'am," said Claire. I wasn't expecting to see you at this briefing. We haven't got much more to go on yet but I'll..."

"Can I have a word outside, Claire?"

"Sure, what's it about?"

"I'd rather not say here. Actually, let's go back to my office."

"Yes, of course." Claire looked around the room. Brian, could you start the briefing and I'll be back in a few minutes."

Claire followed DCI Miller into her small office and closed the door behind her.

"I've just had a call from DCI McGregor at Maryhill. Apparently he's received a request from you to assist with a missing person case – your cousin?"

"Yes, my cousin Anne Duncan went missing on Saturday night and it looks like she's been abducted."

"I'm sorry to hear that Claire but you know the protocol, we don't get involved in cases involving close friends or family. You know that, right?"

"Yes, but I was only offering to help them as I knew Anne and might be able to point them in the right direction. And to be honest, I was never that close with Anne and I haven't seen her for ages so…"

"Well, Dan, I mean DCI McGregor has made it clear that he doesn't want you anywhere near his team's investigation. Is that clear?"

"Yes, but…"

"No Claire, that's an order. You don't get involved! And, anyway, you have enough to deal with here. How are you getting on anyway?"

Just before Claire could answer, the DCI's phone rang.

"Hello, DCI Miller speaking, What? Where? Okay, Secure the area and I'll get there as fast as I can." She looked at Claire. "A body has just been found on the shore at Levengrove Park."

"Oh no, not Anne?" said Claire, her stomach churning at the thought.

"No, it's a male this time, approximately 70 years old so unlikely to be related to your case. I'll take this one but can you spare anyone to assist me with the initial investigation until I get a team together?"

"Not really, I'm going to need my whole team but if it's only for one day then DC Armstrong can assist, I'll let him know?"

"Thanks. I'll arrange to get some extra support; I think we're going to need it."

Claire went back to the incident room where everyone had gathered including DC William Black (Billy) and PC Karen Connelly who had been assigned to assist the team.

"Okay everyone, listen up. Another body has been found. This time it's a 70 year old male so I don't think it's related to this investigation. Jim, can you go with the DCI as she's taking the lead on that one. Hopefully, I'll get you back tomorrow."

She paused to allow Jim to grab his coat and leave the room. "Okay, so hopefully Brian has updated you all on what we know about Lisa Chandler. Next we need to interview all her close friends. We need to find out why she was taken and where she was held. Brian has her address book and will split up the names of her pals between you. We're still waiting for details of the soil analysis to come back from the lab and then we might have more of a clue about where Lisa was kept after she went missing. Any word on the pathologist's report Brian?"

"Not yet, boss."

"Okay, until we do, we hunt down all possible contacts with Lisa. Brian, can you get in touch with Glasgow University and see if you can find out which courses Lisa took while she was there and who were her lecturers, regular classmates and so on? Start with her friend Joyce, Joyce McLeish. She should be able to point you in the right direction. I'll get in touch with Lisa's last employers to see if they have any information which might help." She paused and then faced the rest of the team.

"Alright everyone, we'll meet again first thing tomorrow morning for a further briefing and hopefully we'll have Jim back to help us. Right, you all know what to do, so let's get on with it."

Chapter Fourteen

By the time Claire stopped working that night she was mentally exhausted. As she walked the short distance home she chewed over everything they had learned that day and concluded that she wasn't any closer to solving the case. Claire couldn't help but think that she was missing something - something obvious. Her mind moved on to her missing cousin and she took a mental note to call Maryhill in the morning. The DCI had told her not to get involved but that didn't mean she couldn't be kept informed. DS Bell seemed happy enough to do that much, so with any luck he would be happy to keep her up to date without the DCI getting too upset. DCI Miller had also updated her on the seventy year old male who had been found in the river; apparently the poor man had taken a bad fall before ending up in the water. His body was very badly bruised and some of his clothes were torn. It was being treated as another suspicious death for now pending a full pathology report. The SOC team had been asked to report on their findings at the scene but there was still no evidence to suggest that the two cases were related. The DCI had just put it down to coincidence which didn't sit well with Claire; she didn't like coincidence but had to admit the two cases had nothing in common other than the bodies being found in the river.

As she approached the small terraced house, Claire smiled to herself. She loved the fact that she was not going home to an empty flat after work. Moving in with Peter had been one of her better decisions and it made all the difference to her on days like this.

"Hello, I'm home," she announced, before closing the door behind her. Sally came wandering through to greet Claire, her tail wagging furiously with pleasure. "Hello, girl?" said Claire as she bent down to greet the wee dog. "Where's Peter? Is he in the kitchen? Something smells good."

Claire followed Sally through to the kitchen at the back of the house where she could see Peter standing over the cooker holding a phone in one hand and a wooden spoon in the other; he was stirring a large pot, the contents of which smelled wonderful. Claire was starving and went over to the cooker to see what was cooking.

"Pink pasta, wonderful," she said. Claire loved the so-called pink pasta which Peter made at least once per month. It was a simple but effective pasta dish which was made of cream, tomatoes, chilli powder, mixed herbs and bacon, hence its pink colour. It was simply delicious, especially when served with some toasted garlic bread and salad.

Peter turned to Claire and handed her the phone. "Hi, it's your Mum, she's wants to know if you have found out anything more about Anne?"

Claire reluctantly accepted the phone. "Hello, Mum. Sorry but I've been told to keep away from the case. Yes, I know…but…I'll give Maryhill a call tomorrow morning and hopefully get some more information. Yes, I'm fine. How's Dad keeping? Oh, not so good. Well, give him my love and hopefully he'll feel better soon. Yes, Mum. I will. I promise. Look, I've got to go, Peter has dinner ready and is just about to put it out. Okay. Love you. Bye."

"What's wrong with your Dad?" asked Peter.

"Oh, apparently he's got a bad case of man flu. He'll be fine, probably just a bad cold. You know how men are when they're feeling unwell. It's the end of the world!"

"Ha, ha," said Peter picking up the little dig. "It's just as well I never get ill or I'd never hear the end of it!"

"Yes, well, anyway I'm just going to get freshened up and be down in a minute," said Claire.

"Fine, this'll be ready in a few minutes," said Peter.

As soon as Claire had left the room Peter went over to the drawer where he had hidden the small jewellery box. He had decided not to bother proposing the night before as Claire was too upset over the news about her cousin. However, now that she seemed in better spirits he was not prepared to wait any longer. This was it. This was his chance to pop the question. He was bursting with excitement. Throughout his childhood, Peter had longed for a proper family of his own; his own mother had abandoned him and he was put into local authority care. But that was all past now and he had moved on or so he told himself.

Claire came back downstairs wearing jogging bottoms and a top. Peter didn't care what she was wearing and set about serving the meal on the small kitchen table. He went over to the cupboard and brought out the remains of the red wine which he had opened yesterday but neither of them had felt like finishing after news of her cousin.

"Wine, two nights in a row!" said Claire mockingly.

"Ach, it will just go to waste if we don't finish it," Peter replied casually. Keen not to give her any clue as to what was about to happen.

Claire nodded and they both got stuck into the delicious pasta. Peter finished first and casually took his plate to the sink and went to the drawer and took out the small box. He then knelt down beside Claire who was now wondering what on earth he was up to. Peter held up the box and Claire suddenly realised what he was doing.

"Claire," he said and opened the box to display the small ring. "I know this is unexpected but I've been thinking about it a long time. "I love you Claire Redding. Will you marry me?"

Claire's face went several shades of red; she didn't know what to say. Her heart was racing and finally she caught her breath. "Oh Peter, this is a real surprise! I em...I don't know what to say."

"Say yes, you told me you love me, so..."

"Yes, of course I love you, you know that, I just wasn't expecting this so soon in our relationship."

"It's been just over a year and we are living together, I thought you'd be thrilled but looks like I got it all wrong."

"No, no you didn't. I do love you and I do want to be with you for the rest of my life but marriage, the whole wedding thing! It's not really what I need right now. You know with my work being so hectic and..."

"But it's always going to be like that Claire. I mean, I know Dumbarton is not the crime capital of Europe or even Scotland but you're always busy, always working on something. When will there ever be a right time?"

Claire stopped to think. She knew that she had upset him and that was the last thing she had wanted to do. "Okay, why don't we get engaged and not rush into anything in relation to the wedding. You know, don't set a date yet. How would that be?"

"Well as long as we don't leave it too late, I would like to start a family."

"A family!" Claire almost swallowed her tongue with the sharp intake of breath. "Peter, we have never talked about having a family," she said trying to recover her composure a little.

"Well perhaps we should.   Perhaps now is the perfect time to have that conversation."

Chapter Fifteen

Claire hardly slept a wink that night and was really tired when she finally dragged herself out of bed the next morning. The conversation had not ended well but she had accepted the ring and was officially engaged. However, instead of feeling over the moon, elated even, as she had dreamed she would have when she was a little girl, she didn't. She knew she hadn't handled it well and that was putting it mildly. It was terrible, she was terrible and now she felt terrible.

She looked over at Peter who was still sleeping and she began to weep. She did love him so why didn't she just bite her tongue, enjoy the moment and then deal with the whole big wedding, family thing later. *Why did she need to bring it up last night?* She would apologise, of course, and try to make amends but something deep down in her gut told her that things between her and Peter might never be quite the same again. Something had changed and she knew it was all her fault. He had been the perfect housemate, perfect partner, the perfect lover. His only fault, if you could call it that, was his inherent distrust of all things institutional and who could blame him after his childhood! He often criticised local authorities, which were supposed to look after children in their care. "Getting it Right for Every Child, you're having a laugh. Well you never got it right for me did you," he would shout at the telly whenever a pious social worker or well intentioned teacher mentioned it during an interview. And although, she knew how strongly Peter felt about raising children in care, they hadn't actually talked about whether they both wanted to have children of their own. Well she knew now and that was her biggest conundrum. She didn't want to have any as it would get in the way of her career but she didn't have the courage to tell Peter as she knew now that it could destroy their relationship. *What a mess!*

Chapter Sixteen

Claire removed her engagement ring and put it in her handbag before entering the incident room; her head was still full of thoughts about Peter and she couldn't face all the attention her engagement would attract. So she decided to keep it quiet for now. She had hardly given any thought to the case since last night, which was not like her. She was really out of sorts and DS O'Neill could tell something was wrong as soon as he saw her.

"Everything alright, boss?" he asked.

"What, oh, yes, fine. Okay, let's get going. Let's start with the university. What do you have for us Brian?"

DS O'Neill stood up and took centre stage in front of the large incident board which contained photographs, timelines, list of names and a large map of the Dumbarton area. "I finally managed to get a hold of Joyce McLeish yesterday afternoon. She had been at work all day and had her personal mobile turned off. She was helpful but couldn't really say if there was anyone who had a grudge against Lisa. She has given me details of those classes which she shared with Lisa, names of some of the lecturers that she could remember and pointed me towards some of the other friends which they shared at university. I'll need to follow up on that today. I have also asked the university to send me details of all the classes that she attended, names of fellow students, etc., but it could take a lot of time to get through the full list and not all her lecturers are still working at the university, some have retired, moved on to other colleges, and so on."

"Okay, thanks. What about Lisa's other friends? Anything to report?" she asked.

Brian shook his head. "We've interviewed most of them but all say the same thing, Lisa was a lovely intelligent girl who had her whole life ahead of her. No one could come up with any reason why anyone would want to take her, let alone harm her." He pointed over to Claire's desk in the opposite room. "I've left all the statements for you to review on your desk but as I say, there's nothing there. There's still one or two we need to get a hold of but I'm not hopeful that we will get anything worthwhile."

"Any sign of the pathologist report yet?"

"Yes, boss. I've had a quick look and it pretty much confirms that the cause of death was likely to be starvation/dehydration – there's a whole load of technical information to back that up but you might be more interested in the soil analysis report which also came back late last night." He paused for a reaction.

"Well, don't keep us all in suspense. What did it say!" asked Claire suddenly taking an interest in the case again.

"First of all, the dirt contained particles of volcanic dust."

"What?" Claire was clearly taken aback. "...volcanic dust, we don't have any volcanoes around here, do we?"

"Well none that are active but the whole of Dumbarton is pretty much volcanic or at least it was some 340 million years ago. The Kilpatrick Hills, Dumbuck Quarry, Dumbarton Rock and the Westcliff were all formed by volcanoes at some point. Geologists reckon that the whole of the Strathclyde valley was scraped out by the shifting of a huge glacier during the end of the ice age leaving a series of lochs and rivers behind."

"Well that really narrows it down doesn't it," said Claire unable to contain her sarcasm. "What this says is that Lisa could have been held anywhere in Dumbarton and goodness knows where else, so much for Sherlock Holmes!"

"What?" said Brian now completely confused.

"It's nothing, so what else? You said 'firstly' so there must be something else."

Brian suddenly remembered the best part and smiled. "Oh yes, you're not going to believe this but they also found traces of DNA in the sample." This time Brian knew he really had the attention of the room and everyone reacted to the news by going completely silent, keen to hear more.

"What, we have the DNA of Lisa's abductor?" asked Claire, her excitement obvious for everyone to see and hear. "And you leave this to the end of the briefing to share with us…why?"

"Well no," said Brian hesitant to share the next piece of information.

"So if it's not the abductor's DNA, whose is it?"

"They don't know, it's been sent away for further analysis but they think it is approximately 800 years old."

"What? Does DNA even last that long? Is that a thing?" she asked.

"It must do," said Brian. "Otherwise, they wouldn't have found traces of it in the soil. They were able to confirm that it's human DNA."

"Well that's something at least but I don't see how that could possibly help us find out where Lisa had been held," said Claire thinking out loud.

"You'll need to read the report for more detail but it suggested that it may be possible to trace the ancestry of the DNA, providing the DNA is held on one of the historical databases."

"Really, we might actually be able to identify whose DNA it was?"

"Well, at least the family line. I was reading up on it before you came in," said Brian. "It's amazing what the scientists can do these days. You never know, it might help us find the location. I know it's a long shot but it's worth a try. Oh, I should have mentioned they also provided an estimated cost of the DNA analysis and want authorisation before they proceed."

Claire nodded. "I bet they do. It's not going to be cheap! Great, I'll need to speak to the DCI but it's definitely worth a go as we have very little else to go on." Claire looked round the room properly for the first time and suddenly realised that DC Armstrong had returned to the team.

"Oh hello Jim, nice to have you back. Did you find anything else out about the body of the man that was found in the river?"

"Yes boss, his name was Donald Gallagher."

"Donald Gallagher? Now why does that name sound familiar?" she wondered aloud.

"He's got something to do with looking after Dumbarton Castle, I think," said Brian who was a fount of local knowledge and Claire heavily depended on him for that.

"He's also a local historian and activist," said Jim. "According to the local paper he and one of the local councillors managed to block the opening of a new superstore in the town. He's always in the local press giving comment on that sort of thing."

"That'll be it," said Claire. I knew I'd heard that name before. Sounds like you could have a motive right there, that's if it was a murder! Anything else of interest?"

"Nothing concrete, to be honest. We did find an earring in his jacket pocket which the DCI thinks is curious as Mr Duncan was single. Well, I say single, he was a widower, his wife died a few years ago."

"What about a girl friend?" asked Brian.

Jim laughed at the suggestion. "I hardly think so, he was in his seventies."

"That a bit ageist, Jim," said Claire with a straight face and then burst out laughing.

"Ha, ha," said Jim. "We're still waiting on the forensic report but the DCI now thinks it could have been accidental."

"It seems that way. Okay, let's get back to our case and leave the mysterious case of Mr Duncan's earring to the DCI."

DCI Miller was sitting at her desk when Claire knocked and entered the small office. The DCI was wearing a smart grey jacket and matching skirt with the uniform white blouse underneath. Unusually, she was wearing full make up and her hair looked like she had recently been to the hairdressers.

"Oh, hello Claire, come on in," she said, and gestured to one of two chairs which faced her small desk, which was covered in various buff folders and papers. "I've a press briefing in 10 minutes, so this will need to be quick. It appears our Mr Gallagher was a bit of a local celebrity and the bloody local press are demanding a statement!"

Claire nodded. She knew the DCI only wore full make up when she absolutely had to.

"Yes, we were just hearing an update from Jim in the incident room. He says you found an earring in Mr Gallagher's pocket."

"Yes, it's a bit unusual given his situation. Apparently his sister is coming up from London to do the formal identification. I'll ask her about the earring when she gets here but I'm not confident that she'll be of any help. She didn't appear to be upset at all when I told her that her brother had died. Apparently they hadn't seen each other for years!"

Claire nodded in understanding. "Yes, some families can be like that."

The DCI pointed to the pile of paperwork on her desk. "The pathologist report has come back and it appears that Mr Gallagher had taken a bad fall before he died. Based on the extent of bruising to his head, the pathologist thinks he was probably unconscious before he entered the water so it could have been an accidental death after all. However, it's too early to say for sure and I've still to get the forensic report back. Who knows what that will reveal."

That reminded Claire why she had wanted to see the DCI. "Something interesting has come out of the forensic report from the Lisa Chandler case; apparently the soil analysis taken from the girl's finger nails contains some DNA but they think it's approximately 800 years old?"

"What!" exclaimed DCI Miller, who suddenly took an interest in the conversation and put down the statement that she had been holding.

"That was my reaction too," said Claire. "We were hoping the soil analysis would point us to a location where her body had been held before she died but all it actually pointed to was volcanic dust, which can be found all over Dumbarton apparently. Anyway, the SCO team say it's possible to trace the ancestry of DNA even if it is 800 years old." Claire deliberately didn't mention the fact that they could only trace the ancestry if the DNA was already held on an existing database.

"And you want me to approve the expenditure? Am I right?" asked the DCI getting right to the point.

Claire looked a little sheepish as she knew budgets were tight. They were always tight. "It is a long shot but so far I've got nothing else to go on. This might just help pinpoint the location on the map."

"How much do they want?" asked the DCI.

Claire opened the document she had in her hand and passed the relevant page to the DCI, pointing to the summary of costs at the foot of the page.

"For fuck sake, that's ridiculous," said the DCI.

"I know," said Claire sensing defeat. "But it's all I've got and I didn't want to say this earlier but something in my gut tells me that this could be important."

"Look Claire, I get it. The last thing I want to do is ignore a piece of evidence which might help solve the case but what are we really going to learn from this, even if we are able to identify the DNA? Say we do get lucky and get a trace on the name of someone who was around 800 years ago. How is that going to help us find the location?"

Claire knew this was the crunch question that she couldn't answer. "So I take it that's a no then?" Claire asked.

DCI Miller hesitated for a moment, "Let me read the full report and have a think about it." DCI Miller looked at her watch. "Shit, sorry Claire, I need to go. She grabbed a folder from her desk and practically ran out the room and along the corridor towards the press room where the Chief Superintendent was waiting impatiently for her to start the press conference.

Claire returned to her desk and noticed an A4 envelope, marked for her attention, sitting on the top of her in tray. She looked around the office and held up the envelope for everyone to see. "Did anyone see who delivered this envelope?" she asked.

Brian looked up first and answered. "I think it came through the internal mail." He pointed to the envelope. "See, no stamp. Some detective you are!"

"Alright smart ass," Claire said, and opened the envelope to reveal what appeared to be a photocopy of a police report. There was a sheet of white paper on top which was marked *'Hope this helps. Keep it to yourself. A friend.'*

Claire was intrigued and quickly read the report which she soon realised was the initial sit-rep prepared by Maryhill CID on Anne Duncan's abduction. She read about the white van which had been heading towards Clydebank on the A814 before they lost track of it on CCTV and then went on to read the detailed description of what Anne was wearing when she went missing and a summary of the various statements taken. She noted that Jean McArthur was one of the last people to see Anne alive. She then read the description of the man seen on CCTV in the pub and the ongoing efforts by the Maryhill CID to identify him. Having read the whole report for a second time Claire began to think about who had sent her the report and why? Was it DS Bell, who initially had appeared to be helpful but had then gone to his DCI, who in turn had contacted her DCI and warned Clare to stay away from his investigation? Surely he wouldn't take that type of risk…would he? Claire pondered that for a moment before her thought pattern was interrupted by DS O'Neill.

"Sorry boss, but did the DCI say anything about the DNA? Are we going ahead with the ancestry analysis?"

"Sorry Brian, I should have said when I came back in. She wants more time to think about it. She thinks it's a bit expensive and she's not wrong. We'll just need to follow up on what we have for the time being."

"Thought so," said Brian. "What was in the envelope?"

"Oh nothing, it's…eh…it's personal," she said, desperately trying to think of something to cover her obvious awkwardness.

Brian could tell something was up but again decided to leave it alone. Claire hadn't been herself since she came in that morning. He could tell something was bothering her but didn't want to pry; she would share with him when she was ready. That was her way of doing things and he was more than happy with that.

"Oh right, okay. Well I'm going to pay a visit to Glasgow University and speak to some of the staff who knew Lisa. I'll take Jim with me if that's okay with you or do you have something else for him at the moment?"

"No, nothing that I can think of. I want to go over all the statements and have a proper look at the forensic report again and see if anything new occurs to me."

Brian nodded and then grabbed his coat. He looked around and headed towards Jim who was staring at the large information board in the incident room, which was looking unusually bare for this point in the investigation.

"Come on Jim, we're off to Glasgow University to interview a couple of professors, if that is what they are actually called these days?"

"Aye, some of them might be professors. It all depends on their status within the University." replied Jim. Brian didn't have a clue how the university worked and took Jim's word for it. Jim on the other hand was what Brian considered to be a 'modern copper' and had studied at university before joining the force, just like Claire. Jim had contemplated doing forensic science as a career and had done reasonably well at university but after four years of study he decided that he didn't want to spend his time in a lab; he wanted to be out there, catching the bad guys. He grabbed his coat and followed Brian out of the office.

Chapter Seventeen

Robert was sitting in front of the monitors watching Anne and thinking about his next interview with her. He had just about recovered from the thrill of almost being caught the night before and was delighted by his own genius and speed of mind.

What on earth was Donald Gallagher doing at the castle at that time of night? It was well after closing time and all of the castle staff should have been long gone by then. And although Donald didn't work at the castle it had still been a bit of a shock when he called out to Robert. Anyway, it didn't matter now; he had dealt with Donald and in so doing had given the Police another little headache to add to their current workload. As he sat there, smiling to himself, he relived the memory of his actions over and over again, pleased at his clarity of thought under such pressure. When Gallagher had spotted him, he didn't panic, instead he waved back to him and sauntered nonchalantly over to the old man as if nothing was wrong and then as soon as he got close enough he grabbed hold of his jacket and used his forward momentum to push Gallagher backwards over the edge of the parapet, which was only a few feet away. Unfortunately, the fall onto the shrubs and rocks below had not killed the old man but he had been knocked unconscious which allowed Robert enough time to work out what to do with him. It had taken Robert all his strength to get the old man down to the water's edge, where he held him under the water until he drowned. Thankfully, Gallagher was quite a small man, who clearly looked after himself and therefore was much lighter than Robert. Unsurprisingly the old man did wake up at the shock of the cold water but Robert was far too strong for him and it was over very quickly.

The next part had been a bit trickier as he now had to get rid of the body without being seen. *Robert's* boat was moored at Dumbarton Quay, in the River Leven, which was not that far from the Castle. He dragged the drowned body back up the bank and hid it under some nearby undergrowth. It was dark and there was no artificial lighting to illuminate the area so he was confident that no one would find it during the short while that he was gone. He was completely exhausted by the time he reached his car but the adrenalin flowing through his veins kept him going. He got into his car, which he had left outside the Rock Bowling Club, and quickly drove round to the Quay to fetch his small boat. This was the same boat he had used to dump Lisa's body into the Clyde.

Her death was self-inflicted and was not what he had planned at all. She had not co-operated with him and in the end she refused point blank to eat and drink. Eventually, he gave up making her meals. When she finally succumbed to malnourishment and dehydration, he had no choice but to dispose of her body in the safest way possible. It made sense to use the river as the dirty salt water would surely remove any evidence which could lead to his capture. It had been fascinating for him to watch her die and he had learned something new about human behaviour and about himself. His decision to place the earring, Anne's earring, in Donald's pocket was a master stroke. He was convinced that the less than competent local Police would now conclude that Donald had abducted Anne and that she had probably drowned just like Lisa. They would assume that it was just a matter of time before Anne's body would be found somewhere along the river and, if not, over a period of time she would be forgotten about, just like Lisa. Furthermore, the Police would never discover that Lisa had been a student of his at Glasgow University before he had been dismissed for inappropriate behaviour. The fact that all his students willingly participated in his experimental study was neither here nor there. He had been told that he was lucky to 'just' be sacked and not reported to the Police. He was also warned that he should not apply to work with students ever again as his card was well and truly marked among the university fraternity. However, that was all in the past and what mattered now was that his latest project was successful. Anne, on the other hand, clearly didn't remember him from her time at university which was not surprising as he didn't actually teach her but he certainly noticed her and found out who she was by searching for her details on the university database; she was an ideal candidate for his study. With that thought in mind he decided it was time to speak to Anne again.

Anne was beginning to doubt her earlier confidence that the Police would find her within a day or two and was now seriously concerned about her future.

Yes, on the face of it, her keeper, whose name was clearly not Robert, had been true to his word. She had answered his questions and he had not harmed her. In fact, he had been more than pleasant to her in their recent conversations but she knew that somehow she would need to find a way to escape. However, until that moment came, she would continue to co-operate.

She heard a door opening and waited for her 'keeper' to appear. That's how she now pictured him, as her keeper, keeping her locked up in the small cell, keeping her from the freedom she had enjoyed and had taken for granted, and never would again, if only she could get out of here alive.

"Hello Anne, how are you today?" he asked

"Oh, you know, happy as Larry."

He smiled at her sarcasm and then sat down on the small wooden chair which he carefully placed directly in front of the bed where Anne was sitting with her chin resting on her knees and her arms wrapped around her legs which were folded and tucked into her chest as if she was about to dive bomb into a swimming pool. She relaxed a little and let her slender legs stretch out in front of her.

"So, what are we going to chat about today?" she asked with feigned enthusiasm.

"Do you believe in God, Anne?" he asked.

"Wow, that's a big question. Are you serious? Why on earth would you want to know that?"

"As I have said before, I'm interested in finding out who you really are, what makes you tick, so it's important to me to find out as much as I can about your inner beliefs and social drivers."

"Social drivers, what do you mean by that?" she asked.

"Yes social drivers, you know - what motivates us to do what we do, be who we want to be? What is the internal driving force that makes us who we really are?"

"Well, that's very deep, I hope I don't disappoint," she said.

"There's no chance of that," he said. "You just need to be completely honest and not just with me, with yourself. It can be really enlightening and rewarding if you just allow yourself to open up to the absolute truth, say what you really feel, reveal what you truly believe and do not conform to the norm and say what others want you to say. Do you understand?"

Anne sat there quietly contemplating what he had just said. She felt that for the first time he had opened up to her and revealed a bit of his true self, and if she was being completely honest with herself she did think what he said made a lot of sense. She just couldn't understand where all this questioning was going and that scared her.

Okay, I get it," she said. "So, do I believe in God? Hmmn! To be honest, I don't really know what to believe. Don't get me wrong, I want to believe there is a God. I want to believe there is life after death and that there is a 'heaven' where you get to meet your loved ones again, forever and ever, Amen. But, I just find it very hard to understand how any of that could be possible never mind half the rubbish that is printed in the bible. You know, all that guff about the Earth being created in seven days, Adam and Eve…and all that creationist nonsense. Science has proven that all that stuff is fiction. So where do you draw the line between the facts and fiction when you read the bible? I don't think it's possible to cherry pick the bits of the bible that suit you and ignore the other bits. It's either all or nothing for me."

"So, you don't believe then?" he asked, prompting her to continue.

"I certainly don't believe in the mysterious benevolent all powerful, omnipotent God of creation that lives in a heaven surrounded by angels playing harps and trumpets and God knows what else!" she responded sharply.

"So, now we're getting down to the good stuff. What do you believe in, Anne?"

"Oh, I don't know. It's all so confusing," she said. "I suppose I do believe that there was a man called Jesus who lived over 2000 years ago, but was he the Son of God? Was he sent to Earth to put us all straight and tells the Jews that they had got it all wrong? That everyone should follow him and live by his new rules, sorry God's new rules, and not the rules which Moses allegedly brought down from the mountain on tablets of stone from God?"

"That's Interesting," said Robert.

"What's interesting?" asked Anne who was now fully engaged in the conversation.

"The fact that you need to see or hear evidence before you can truly believe in anything. That's not uncommon, of course. In fact, it's the normal response in terms of human behaviour." He paused for a moment to reflect on his next question.

"Tell me Anne, do you think you are easily influenced by external factors. Do you believe everything that people tell you, people who are supposed to be wise or at least wiser than you are, like our educators, or are you a free thinker?"

"Well I'd like to think that I'm a free thinker," she said, again intrigued where this line of questioning was heading.

"Okay then, let's test that assertion a little. Let's start with your views on creationism since you are adamant that the Earth couldn't be built in a day. How much do you really know about how the Earth was formed?"

Her back was up now and she was confident she was on solid ground. "Well everyone knows about the big bang theory so clearly God did not create the Earth and the stars on the first day. That's just wrong."

Robert grinned at her and replied. "Would it surprise you to know that those same scientists estimate that it took approximately three minutes for the Earth and all the stars within our universe to be formed?"

"What, no, that can't be right and even if it is, which it isn't, it still means the Earth was formed by a 'Big Bang' and not God."

"True, but it makes you think a bit differently about it, doesn't it. After all, the Big Bang Theory is just that, a theory formed by a group of scientists looking for answers. No one can prove it actually happened, in the same way that no one can prove that there is or isn't a God? What we have to take into account is that when the bible was first written all those years ago, there was no science to explain what might have happened but nevertheless even the description in the bible could be argued to describe the big bang theory and let's face it, the timeframe used in the bible wasn't actually that far from current thinking, was it? And who's to say that the Big Bang, if indeed that is how the Earth was created, was not the work of God."

Anne was stumped. She hadn't expected the discussion to turn into a full blown debate, one of which she was clearly ill prepared for and more importantly she was losing. Robert could tell by her demeanour that he had dampened her fuse a little and was keen to re-ignite her enthusiasm.

"The point I'm trying to make is that we are all influenced by what we are told and sometimes, perhaps more importantly, we are influenced by what they don't tell us, especially the so called educators. I know, I used to…" He managed to stop himself completing the sentence; he was enjoying the conversation so much he got carried away.

He started again. "This is what actually interests me more than the answers to the big philosophical questions that we're discussing. In particular, how easily can the human mind be influenced, changed, directed to think a certain way without us even being aware of it. People like Paul McKenna are brilliant at it. Anyway, let's explore the God question a little further, shall we? You mentioned that you believed there was a person called Jesus on Earth. I assume that's because you believe that there is enough evidence that he did exist?"

"Yes, that and the fact that I can't understand how it could be possible for so many countries in all parts of the world to have heard of him without there ever being a real Jesus in the first place. Not to mention that there are many letters written by his disciples and others just after his death, which all testify to his existence. However, whether or not he actually performed miracles including bringing the dead back to life, is a completely different question as none of that stuff can ever be proven.

However, his message of love and peace has spread throughout the world and is still alive today…perhaps that's the real miracle. Anyway, I really don't see how it's possible for all that to have happened if Jesus wasn't a real person."

Robert considered her response carefully as there was a lot of information to digest. "Well, first of all you are correct to say that there is evidence of his existence but did you know that there is actually more evidence to prove the existence of Jesus Christ than any other person in ancient history?"

"No, I didn't know that," said Anne. "So how do you know all this stuff? Did you read it in books by so called educators?"

"Touché, and now you're beginning to understand the point I was making earlier and are now beginning to question things you thought you knew as fact. I don't really care about whether you believe there's a God or not, I'm more interested to discover why you believe or don't believe. Anyway, this conversation is going much better than I had hoped so let's take it to another level. Let's discuss the existence of good and evil!"

Chapter Eighteen

When Brian and Jim returned to the station, Claire was sitting at her desk staring into space.

"Hi boss, anything new?" said Brian hopefully.

Claire came quickly out of her daze and shook her head, blowing the air from her lungs in total exasperation. "Nothing, what about you?"

"Same," said Brian. "We did manage to get the complete list of names of all the lecturers Lisa would have had contact with. I'll put them on the incident board for all to see. We also managed to interview some of them but they could barely remember her. No real surprise there given the number of students they see each year. And, as I said before one or two have since left the university. Oh, one of them was sacked for inappropriate behaviour – a Professor William Fairbairn-Smythe. Nothing criminal as such but it was enough to justify them getting rid of him. I'll run his name through the database in case anything is flagged. Shouldn't take long with a name like that. There can't be many Fairbairn-Smythes around," he joked.

"Okay, thanks Brian. What was his subject?"

Brian hesitated and took out his little book to check. "Oh, yes here it is, he was a professor of psychology."

"Right Jim, you can do a bit of research tomorrow to see if we can track him down elsewhere, you know at another university or college but don't spend too much time on it. I really don't expect it to lead anywhere."

"Right boss, I'll get onto it first thing in the morning. He looked at his watch. "Is it okay if I head off home now or is there something I can do before I go?" asked Jim.

Claire looked at Brian, who nodded in response. "Yes, sure thing Jim, it's all quiet here at the moment."

"Thanks boss, I'll see you both tomorrow, bright and breezy," said Jim as he grabbed his coat and marched off out of the room.

Claire smiled at Jim as he left, but her smile quickly disappeared at the thought of having to go home; she had never felt this way before and was absolutely dreading it. Peter was clearly still upset when she left home that morning. He barely said a word to her and she hoped that he would be in a better mood when she finally worked up the courage to face him again.

She decided to take another look at the report on Anne's disappearance before going home. She hoped to have something positive to tell her Aunt Cathy although on first reading it was clear that Maryhill were having as much luck with Anne's case as she was with Lisa's. She read the report for the second time with a more critical eye and realised that there were some gaps in their approach to the investigation. The most obvious one related to the image of the suspect captured by CCTV. Although the suspect's face was not caught on camera, he could have been spotted by one of the girls in Anne's group and perhaps they would be able to give a physical description of his face, if they had noticed him. She could see from the report that they all had been questioned and given statements but nowhere did it suggest that they had been shown the CCTV image of the suspect. Maybe that was the next step for Maryhill CID, to go back to them and ask the question, but she didn't want to leave it to chance. She had to know. Claire grabbed her coat and headed for the door.

"See you tomorrow, Brian."

Brian looked up. "Bit early for you isn't it," he said looking at his watch. "What's the occasion? Peter got something nice in the oven?"

"What? No, no, nothing like that. I've got a personal appointment, that's all," she said, and strode out of the office. She didn't like telling lies to Brian but it was best if he didn't know about her looking into the Maryhill investigation.

"Okay, see you in the morning!" said Brian to an empty room. He sat there staring at the door.

Something was wrong with Claire, he could sense it.

Claire knew fine well that she was going to get into trouble if the DCI found out that she was getting involved in Anne's disappearance but that was a risk she was prepared to take. She had to know that all leads were being pursued and strode into Maryhill station determined to find out. She recognised the desk sergeant from her time there before and walked right up to him.

"Hi Bob. Is DS Bell in the office?" she asked hopefully.

"Oh hi Claire, long time no see. How's the fast lane in Dumbarton?" he joked.

"Ha ha, very funny! Well, is Andy in?" she asked showing just a little frustration in her tone.

"No, Andy's not here, you've just missed him. DC McWilliams is still there though. Shall I get her for you?"

"No, it's okay. I'll just go through and introduce myself, I do know where I'm going."

"Of course you do, on you go." He pressed the buzzer and the door into the station opened automatically.

DC McWilliams was just leaving the CID office when she saw Claire striding towards her.

"Hello, can I help you?" asked DC McWilliams.

"Hi, DI Claire Redding, Dumbarton. I'm looking for DC McWilliams."

The young DC's face dropped in shock. "What, how did you know it was me?"

At first Claire was confused and then the penny dropped. "Ah, you're my secret friend."

The young DC grabbed Claire's arm and pulled her into the nearest empty office. "What are you doing here? You'll get us both into trouble," she said and closed the door behind her. "The DCI will have kittens if he finds out you're here."

"I know, and sorry, but there's something I need to ask about the investigation that DS Bell is running."

"Okay, but not here, it's too risky."

"Okay, where?" asked Claire.

"There's a wee café over the road. I can meet you there in 5 minutes."

"That's great, can I get you a coffee or tea?" asked Claire.

"Coffee, no milk, no sugar," said DC McWilliams.

Claire headed straight back out of the station and thanked Bob for his help as she passed by his desk on the way to the exit. She spotted the café, crossed the road and entered the door to the ring of a bell which announced the arrival of customers. She approached the counter where an elderly looking lady, wearing an apron and a frown on her face was waiting.

"Can I have two black coffees please?" asked Claire.

"Is that to go?" the woman asked.

"No, sitting in thanks," said Claire.

"Well, we close in 15 minutes so you'll need to be quick. Expecting someone else are you. Two coffees?" she asked.

"Yes," said Claire. My friend's just coming, she's..."

"A police officer?" asked the woman. "I saw you cross the road. Are you one of them then?"

Claire didn't know how to respond to that. "No, I'm a secret informant on a secret mission so don't tell anyone," she whispered and winked at the old woman.

"Aye, right and Ah'm the First Minister. You're Police through and through. It's obvious."

Claire was just about to respond when DC McWilliams entered the café. Claire turned round and pointed to a table in the corner. "Be with you in a minute. Nicola here is just getting our coffees. Is that right Nicola?"

The woman glared at Claire and poured hot coffee into the two cups she had placed on the counter. "That'll be three quid and we close in ten minutes."

Claire paid for the coffees and sat down beside DC McWilliams.

"Nicola?" asked DC McWilliams.

"Long story," said Claire. "Anyway thanks for sending me the report...eh...DC McWilliams, is it?"

"Call me Alice. And you're welcome. When DS Bell, Andy, told me that Anne Duncan was your cousin, I felt really bad that the DCI didn't want you to be involved."

"Yeah, he called my DCI and told her to keep me away from the case," said Claire. "Anyway, the reason why I felt I had to speak to Andy was I wanted to make sure that you were going to share the image of the suspect at the bar with Anne's friends, the ones who were in the club that night."

Alice nodded. "It was me who spotted him after spending hours of going through all the CCTV footage. I know that Andy certainly asked for the photo to be circulated to staff and regulars in the pub. You know, to see if anyone recognised him but I don't think he thought about Anne's friends. Shit! Why didn't I think of that! It's bloody obvious."

"Look I'm not here to criticise or comment on what your team is doing but can you make sure that it happens now. I doubt if anyone will know who he is but perhaps we might get a better description of his face. You know; something we can maybe run through the face recognition software?"

"I'll get right on that when I get back to the station."

"Thanks. What else have you found?"

"Well, we now know that the vehicle's plates were cloned. We managed to get a view of the plate on the van and ran it through the system. The plates were registered to a similar small van but it was a different make and model. Interestingly, the vehicle which was cloned is registered in Dumbarton," said Alice.

"And according to the report, the van was heading towards Clydebank. So, it's possible that it was actually heading back to Dumbarton," said Claire thinking out loud.

"That's what we are now thinking," said Alice.

"Have you spoken with the owner of the cloned vehicle yet?"

"That's what Andy's doing now. Funny that, he's in Dumbarton and you are here," she said.

Claire didn't respond. She was now deep in thought.

"Well if that's all I'd better get back to the office before I'm missed," said Alice. She gulped down the coffee and stood up to go. "Thanks for the coffee."

"Will you let me know how Andy gets on with the owner of the vehicle?" asked Claire.

"Will do, Claire. I think our DCI was going to tell your boss that we are now looking for a suspect in your area. You never know, they might even let you get involved after all."

"There's no chance of that," said Claire, who then stood up and turned to the woman behind the counter. "Goodbye Nicola."

"Fuck off!" she responded and stuck two fingers up in the air to re-inforce the sentiment.

Both police officers burst into laughter and left the café giggling like a pair of teenagers. They exchanged telephone numbers and went their separate ways.

Claire decided to go back to the office before going home. She had sent a text to Peter from her car and told him she was going to be a bit late. He had responded with one word 'okay', which was not like him. There was no kiss added to it as usual so Claire assumed she was still in the bad books.

When she got back into the office, she turned on her laptop and signed into the Police Scotland network to check for messages. Top of the list was one from the DCI asking Claire for a quick update on the case. Instead of typing a response, she decided to go and see if the DCI was till around.

Claire knocked the door to the DCI's office and popped her head round the door. "Are you free for a quick update, Ma'am?"

The DCI was sitting at her desk and Claire could tell from the frown on her face that the DCI was very angry. The DCI was holding a copy of the local paper in both hands; her grip crushing the edges of the paper. "Have you seen the fucking headlines?"

"No, what are they saying now?" asked Claire.

"River of Death! The bastards didn't listen to a word I said at that press conference."

"Not very original though. Is that not the headline they use every time a body is found in the Clyde," said Claire trying to take the heat out of the situation. She wasn't looking forward to telling the DCI that she was no further forward with the Lisa Chandler case.

"So, any progress with the case?" asked the DCI.

"We've spoken to all her friends and spoken to most of her lecturers at university but nothing. There was one of them who had been sacked for inappropriate behaviour and DC Armstrong is trying to track him down but even if we do, we have nothing to connect him to the case."

DCI Miller nodded slowly as if she had anticipated the response. "I'm not making much progress with the Gallagher case either. The Chief Super is demanding results so we're going to need to get a break on one of the two bodies soon or we'll both be in the shit." She paused for a moment and then made a decision. "Go ahead with the DNA analysis, I'll find the money somewhere."

"Thanks, as I said, it won't identify the killer but could help us find out where she was held," said Claire.

"I know," said the DCI. "Oh, I meant to tell you. Maryhill has been in touch. Apparently the van involved in your cousin's abduction was registered in Dumbarton."

"Really!" said Claire, feigning her surprise.

"Yes, but it looks like the plates were cloned."

"Oh, did Maryhill say who the real plates are registered to? We might be able to help them find the owner?"

"No, they didn't mention the name and I didn't ask. It's not our case Claire. They were just letting me know as a matter of courtesy."

"I know. I just thought we could help…"

"I know it's your cousin and I know you want to help but DCI McGregor has made it very clear that he doesn't want you anywhere near the case. And anyway, they are doing better than we are with our two mysterious deaths?"

Claire knew when to back off and now was the time so she changed tact. "Have you had the forensic report back on your Mr Gallagher yet?"

"Yes, I was just about to go through it before you arrived," said the DCI and pressed the return key on the laptop to bring up the report again and didn't look up again.

Claire took that as her cue to leave. "Okay, I'll leave you in peace." She turned to go out the door.

"Oh, there was one thing more I learned about the case which is bothering me," said the DCI.

"What's that?" asked Claire.

"You know that earring we found in Gallagher's pocket?"

"Yes, you were going to ask his sister about it," said Claire.

"I did and she didn't recognise it."

Claire paused for a moment to think. "What if the earring belonged to Lisa Chandler? What if Gallagher was the one who dumped her body in the river but accidentally managed to drown himself in the process."

DCI Miller nodded her head and added to the line of thought. "And what if both deaths were accidental? You know, he abducts the girl, she refuses to eat, he gets concerned so decides to take her somewhere…" She stopped herself before finishing the sentence. "No, forget that, it's total speculation but it's certainly worth finding out if the earring belongs to Lisa Chandler."

"Where is the earring now?" asked Claire.

"Still with forensics I imagine, I've just received their report." The DCI could read Claire's mind. "I have the SOC photographs of the earring on my laptop. I'll send them over to you. Get it printed and go and see the Chandlers now. Don't waste any time. If it's Lisa's earring, get your whole team back in here pronto. Stuff the overtime! We might be able to clear this whole mess up by morning."

"Will do," said Claire now buzzing with excitement and practically ran back to her office.

Claire headed out to Helensburgh with an enlarged copy of the photograph of the earring sitting on the passenger seat of her squad car. She was bursting at the seams with excitement but knew she would need to play down the situation with the Chandlers and not build up any expectations. Even if the earring did belong to Lisa there was still a lot of police work to do to prove that Gallagher had adducted the girl. They hadn't proven anything yet. With that thought in mind, Claire started to plan the rest of the investigation as if Gallagher was now the main suspect. She would get a warrant to search his house, car, – did he have a boat? How did he get her body into the river? If he did drown accidentally then how did it happen? She had lots of unanswered questions which her team would be tasked to investigate as soon as she got back to the office.

The journey to Helensburgh had only taken 15 minutes; the road was quiet and she got a clean run with no slow tractors or lorries to hold her up. Claire composed herself and went up to the door and rang the bell. PC Jenny Barnes opened the door.

"Hi Jenny," said Claire. "I need to speak to Mr and Mrs Chandler, are they in?"

"Yes, of course, come on in. They are through in the kitchen eating right now. Come into the living room and I'll let them know you are here."

"Thanks," said Claire, who did as she was asked and went in to the living room and sat down.

The Chandlers came into the room, both clearly eager to find out what was going on. Had something happened? Had they found the killer?

Claire stood up as they entered the room and asked them to sit down. She apologised for disturbing them during their meal and took the photograph and passed it to Mr Chandler. "Do either of you recognise the earring in this photograph?" she asked.

Mr Chandler looked at the picture and then handed it to his wife. "Why, is it Lisa's?" asked Mr Chandler. "Where did you find it? Do you have a suspect?"

Claire ignored the questions. "Please look carefully at the photograph and let me know if you recognise it?"

Mrs Chandler handed it back to Claire, "Sorry I've never seen it before?"

"Are you sure?" asked Claire and passed it back to Mr Chandler.

"Sorry, I don't recognise it either," said Mr Chandler.

Claire could not hide the disappointment on her face. She was gutted. She stood up to leave and took the photograph back. "I'm sorry to have bothered you both. Have a good evening." She left the room and turned towards the door quickly followed by PC Barnes who was less than pleased.

"What was that all about?" asked Jenny closing the outer door behind her just enough to muffle the conversation.

"Sorry Jenny, perhaps I should have warned you before I got here. We found this earring on another body which was found dead in the river."

"Another body?" she exclaimed.

"Yes, and clearly we were hoping that the two were connected but looks like we were totally wrong. I was wrong, it was my idea and now I'm going to have to tell the DCI!"

"Good luck with that," said Jenny.

When Claire got back to the car she decided to call the DCI with the bad news. They were back to square one. Although the DCI was clearly not happy with the news she didn't lose her temper. The conversation ended with the two officers agreeing to pursue the DNA analysis, as they had nothing else to go on. Claire took a mental note to tell Brian first thing in the morning. She was knackered and decided it was time to go home. She was absolutely dreading it but nevertheless she texted Peter to say that she was on her way home. Again the response was just 'okay' – no kiss.

Chapter Nineteen

Claire entered the door to the small terraced house and was pleased when Sally came bounding through the narrow hallway to greet her. *At least Sally hadn't fallen out with her*, she thought, as she entered the hall and dumped her coat and bag on the coat stand.

"Hello Sally," she said and bent down to hug the wee dog. "Come on, let's see if your master's still speaking to me?"

"I heard that," said Peter from the kitchen.

"Looks like he is," said Claire to Sally, somewhat relieved. Claire really wasn't sure what to expect and popped her head around the kitchen door. "Is it safe to come in?" she asked sheepishly.

"Of course it is, you dafty," said Peter.

Claire came all the way into the room. "I'm sorry Peter, you know, about last night! I've been thinking about it all day and…"

"It's alright. I'm over it now. Yes, I was upset last night…"

"And this morning," she added.

"Yes, fair enough, and this morning but we do need to talk about it," he said, turning towards her and making eye contact.

Claire took a deep breath in and let out a long silent sigh before speaking. "Yes, we need to talk. Can we leave it until after dinner though, I'm famished? What's for tea?"

Peter just laughed at the quick change of subject. "Well, as I didn't know what time you would be home I've just prepared some salad, if that's alright. It'll only take a few minutes to put out."

"Perfect, can I help?" she offered.

"Sure, it's all in the fridge. I'll get the plates and you get the food."

The meal had gone well and both had managed to avoid the thorny subject of having a family but now that they were sitting in the front room Claire knew it was time to clear the air. Sally had snuggled into Peter on the couch so Claire decided to sit on the chair opposite him.

"Before we get in to it," said Peter. "Is there any news about your cousin, Anne?"

"Shit, I was supposed to phone Aunt Cathy with an update, I'd better go…"

"No, not now, can you leave it until after we've finished? I have something to say and I need to get it off my chest," said Peter.

He looked at Claire's hands and suddenly went silent; his whole demeanour changed. "Where's your ring?"

"What?" said Claire who suddenly realised that her ring was still in her bag. *Shit! Shit! Shit!* "Eh'm, it's in my handbag. I...I took it off to wash my hands at work and put it in my bag for safe keeping. I must have forgotten to put it in back on. I'll go and get..."

"Don't bother. It's clearly not that important to you."

"What? No, of course it's important to me Peter. I love you, you know that."

"What did your colleagues say about your engagement? I bet they were thrilled."

Claire froze, she knew she had been caught out and decided she couldn't tell any more lies. "They don't know I'm, I mean, that we're engaged."

"What!"

Claire could see that tears were beginning to form in his eyes. She knew she had hurt him. "I'm sorry Peter. We're in the middle of a big case and I didn't want to distract them with news of my engagement. I'll announce it when the time is right."

"You'll announce it when the time is right," Peter repeated slowly. "And when exactly will that be, you're always working on a case Claire?"

Claire knew it was pointless arguing, she had screwed up big time and there was no defence. Tears started to form in her eyes. "I'm sorry, I've messed up. I mess everything up."

Peter was just about to respond when the telephone rang. "Christ, who can that be at this time of night?" he said under his breath. He got up and stormed out into the hall to answer the phone.

Claire sat in the front room, tears streaming from her face. How could she have been so stupid! She blamed herself completely; this was all her doing. After his initial upset, Peter had come round and was willing to talk. They were just about to clear the air and move on, but now! Now it couldn't get any worse.

Peter came back into the room. "Claire. It's your mum. She says your dad is really ill. He's has been taken into hospital with some sort of respiratory infection. It seems really bad. She's with him in the hospital now and has asked if you could meet her there.

"Oh God, I better go," said Claire.

"I'll drive you if you want?" said Peter.

Claire looked at him, her eyes expressing a thousand emotions. The old Peter was back. The lovely man, who she had met in a car park and had fallen head over heels in love with, was still there. She nodded slowly and then hugged him as tight as she could. "I love you Peter Macdonald."

She looked down, only to see Sally at their feet, tail wagging furiously. "Oh, what about Sally, we can't leave her here on her own at this time of night."

"It's fine. I'll take her round to Andy Fraser. He's looked after her before; remember when I was arrested by your lot."

"How could I forget!" she said, still feeling a little guilty that he had been caught up in a mess at her work and not in a good way.

"Anyway, I'm sure Andy will be happy to take her again; he actually said so the last time."

"Okay, good, let's go," said Claire.

Peter and Claire arrived at the Queen Elizabeth University Hospital in Glasgow a few minutes after 9 o'clock. The roads were quiet and they had made it there in only 25 minutes without breaking any speed limits on the way. As they approached the massive new hospital they were both impressed by the scale of it; not to mention its ultra-modern design. It really was like something out of a movie that had been set in the future, except this was 2020 and the hospital was very real.

They quickly parked their car in the massive car park and made their way to the main reception where they were directed to Ward 1. They followed signs to the Acute Recovery Unit – Respiratory Care and went straight to the nurses' reception area. One of the nurses told Claire that her father had been put into a private room and that her mother was with him.

When Claire entered the small room she could see her mum sitting with her dad who was lying in bed, wired up to a machine and had a face mask over his face.

"Hello Mum," said Claire as she approached the bed. Peter decided to stay back and let Claire and her mum have some privacy.

"How is he doing?" whispered Claire. She could see that her dad was sleeping and didn't want to disturb him.

"Oh Claire, thank God you're here. The doctor says he's stable. They're giving him oxygen and have taken some blood for testing. They're not sure but think it's some sort of virus. Oh, but what a fright I got, I honestly thought he was dying. I've never been so scared."

"I bet you were. Thank God he's okay now though. You did the right thing calling an ambulance."

"Yes, well he's stable at least but he's not out of the woods yet. The doctor was very concerned when he first arrived. He gave Dad a sedative and something to reduce his temperature, that's what knocked him out. He couldn't stop coughing at home and was really struggling to breathe."

"That sounds terrible, Mum. Are you alright?" asked Claire.

"I am now that you're here love." She stood up and hugged Claire and noticed Peter standing at the back of the room. "And you Peter, it's good to have you both here."

"How are you Mrs Redding?" said Peter slowly approaching the bed.

"You can call me Barbara. After all you are practically one of the family now. It was good of you come."

"Don't be silly. It was the least I could do. I'm just glad Mr Redd...John... is okay," he replied.

Claire reached into her handbag and pulled out the small ring which had nestled at the bottom of her bag and put it on her finger. "Oh Mum, I almost forgot. We have some good news for you. Peter and I got engaged," Claire said, looking at Peter and smiling.

"What! Oh, that's wonderful news. Your dad will be absolutely delighted. I can't wait to tell him when he wakes up." She hugged Claire again and then went over to Peter and hugged him just as hard. "Congratulations. I'm so pleased for you both.

"Are you allowed to stay here overnight Mum?" asked Claire.

"What? Oh yes, it's one of the perks of having individual rooms but just one person is allowed to stay at a time, I'm afraid."

"Oh, that's okay. The main thing is that he's stable and in safe hands," said Claire.

"Yes, thank God for that. Oh, I meant to ask, is there any news about Anne?"

Claire nodded. "They still haven't found her but there have been some developments; we're trying to identify the man we think was responsible for her abduction."

"Really, have you told your Aunt Cathy? The poor soul is distraught with worry. We all are. I can't imagine how I would cope if that happened to you. It makes my stomach churn just thinking about it."

"No, not yet, I was going to call her tonight but then you called about dad and that took priority. I'll call her from the car on my way home but I hate to say it, it's not looking good Mum. Even if we do find the basta…, the man who took her, we have no idea if she's still alive." As soon as she said the last part, she regretted it and quickly back tracked. "But, we have no reason to think that she's dead either."

"Well whatever you do, don't say all that to your Aunt Cathy. She's bad enough as it is. Look love, I know you've just got here and I'm very grateful but your dad is fine. I'll stay with him and let you know if anything changes overnight. Why don't you two go home and make that call to Cathy?"

"Are you sure Mum?"

"Yes love. You need to go to work in the morning, I don't. I'll call if anything happens. Thanks again for being here. It was just the shock of being in the ambulance, you know."

"Well, if you're sure," said Claire.

"Yes, now off you go and I'll speak to you in the morning."

After saying their farewells and even more hugging, Peter and Claire retraced the route out of the huge hospital and found their car in the almost empty car park. Claire called her Aunt Cathy as promised and gave her a brief version of the update. Claire promised to keep her Aunt informed of any developments and reassured her that the Maryhill team was doing everything possible to find Anne.

By the time they got home it was well after 10 o'clock and Peter knew it was too late to continue their earlier conversation, not to mention insensitive, given the emotional rollercoaster that Claire had just gone through with her father. However, he was also happy that she had announced their engagement. He wasn't sure if she was going to do it tonight and would have completely understood if she hadn't, given the circumstances, but she had, and that had helped to make up for her taking the ring off at work. They both went to bed still speaking which was better than the previous night.

Chapter Twenty

At 6.30 am Claire woke to the sound of her alarm clock. She'd had a better sleep than the previous night, felt completely refreshed and decided to go for a quick run before going to work. She loved running and often planned the day ahead during that 30 minutes of peaceful clarity which running allowed her. She thought about the investigation and what needed to happen to progress matters but she also knew that she had to announce her engagement to the team. That was the bit she wasn't looking forward to; she really hated all that fuss. When she got back home Peter was up and was getting ready to take Sally out on her morning walk. She quickly had her shower and decided to call her mum before she went to work. Her mum told her that her dad had woken early but the cough had returned. Her mum also told her that he was still on oxygen as that helped and she was waiting for the consultant to see him at about 10 am. Her mum told her that the news of the engagement had given him a boost and he seemed much more like his old self this morning, which was positive. Claire was relieved to hear that he was feeling better and ended the call by asking her mum to call her if anything changed.

Claire arrived at the police station wearing the engagement ring and headed straight to the office to brief the team. Brian and Jim were already in the incident room when she arrived and it didn't take Brian long to notice the sparkling ring. Claire spotted him staring at her hand. "Yes, it's an engagement ring, before you ask," said Claire.

"Congratulations, boss," said Brian.

On hearing the news, Jim got up. "Congratulations boss, let's have a closer look then?" he said pointing to the ring.

Claire raised her hand to show off the ring.

"That must have cost a pretty penny or two!" said Jim. "Just as well Peter earns plenty, eh!"

Claire didn't respond to that remark. It hadn't even occurred to her that the ring would be expensive. At that point, the two other members of the team entered the room.

PC Connelly was first to comment. "What's all the fuss then?" she asked.

"The boss has got engaged, Karen," piped up Jim. "You should see the ring, it's a beauty!"

The young female police officer approached DI Redding to get a closer look at the ring. "Oh …my… God! That must have cost a fortune. You're so lucky! Tell me, did he get down on one knee when he proposed? Was it very romantic?"

This line of questioning was exactly what Claire wanted to avoid. "Yes, he did get down on one knee and yes, it was very romantic. He prepared a meal and surprised me with the ring at the dining table. Now, you have all the details so let's get back to work, shall we?"

Brian just sat there grinning like a Cheshire cat and said nothing. He knew that something was up with Claire and all was clear now. He also knew that she hated all the attention that news of the engagement would bring and smiled at her obvious discomfort. He had met Peter a couple of times and recalled their first encounter in the Police station when Peter had been falsely arrested in connection with a spate of burglaries. That was until Claire arrived on the scene; she was the one who solved the case and in so doing had put her own life at risk. He barely knew her back then and he regretted that he had not believed her when she tried to defend Peter's innocence but that was all history now and their relationship had grown stronger and stronger over the past year as they had learned to trust each others' instincts. They were a good team and they both knew it. And so, he was really pleased that she and Peter were together now and had made the relationship more permanent. He also knew how important it was to go home after a bad day and have someone to talk to, someone to share the heavy burden of being a police officer. He decided that when things quietened down, if they ever did, that he would invite Peter and Claire over to his house for a meal. His wife, Agnes, had said as much and now that the pair were engaged the time seemed right to have them both over to meet the family.

Claire went over to the incident board, had a quick look and turned to face the team. "Okay first things first, the DCI has given the go ahead for the DNA analysis. Brian, can you get onto that right away and tell them it's urgent."

Brian nodded. "That's great boss."

"Jim, you already know what I want. Look into the missing lecturer and see if you can get a current address. Billy, I want you and Karen to go through every statement taken and cross reference them. If possible I want to try to pull together a complete timeline of events and flag up anything which appears to be wrong or contradictory."

It was clear from Billy's face that he wasn't too enamoured with the task.

Claire picked up the signal and added. "I know it's going to be time consuming and boring but you never know what it might reveal. We have little else to go on."

Billy nodded in silence.

"Brian, once you've organised the DNA stuff, I want us to go through all the forensic evidence again. Leave no stone unturned."

Right boss," said Brian and turned to the rest of the team. "Right, you all heard the boss, let's get to it."

Claire and Brian spent most of the morning raking through the forensic report desperately trying to find something new, something they had missed which would lead them to Lisa's abductor but so far had come up blank. Brian went over to see how Billy and Karen were getting on with the timeline while Claire started to go through some of her emails. It was only then that she noticed one marked urgent. It was from DC McWilliams and simply said 'Call me on my mobile, Alice.'

Claire went out of the room to make the call in private. After a few rings, DC McWilliams picked up the call.

"Hello?" asked Alice, she would normally give her name but she didn't recognise Claire's number.

"Hi Alice, It's Claire. Are you free to speak?"

"Give me a minute," said Alice, who immediately left her office to find a private room to take the call.. "Hi, thanks for calling back. There's something I thought you would want to know. You know the cloned plates we were tracking?"

"Yes," said Claire.

"Well it turns out the original plates were registered to a Dumbarton man called Donald Gallagher. Does that name mean anything to you?"

Claire went silent.

"Hello, Claire, are you still there?"

"Yes, yes, I know of him but he's dead. We found his body in the Clyde."

"I know. The reason why I'm calling is to let you know that there's going to be a meeting between my DCI and your DCI to decide who is taking the case forward."

"What! When?" asked Claire.

"Some time this afternoon, I think. I don't have the exact time as I'm not involved."

"Right, I'll go and speak to DCI Miller. I want to be part of that meeting."

"No, you can't do that. You're not supposed to know about it, remember."

"Okay, leave it with me, I'll think of something to get involved without revealing that I know about it."

There was a pause at the end of the line as Alice began to question if she completely trusted Claire or not. "Okay, but please be careful."

"I will, so don't worry," said Claire. "Is that all?"

"Yes, eh I mean no, you were right."

"Right about what? Claire asked.

"About checking if any of Anne's friends saw the man in the bar; one of the girls, Brenda Dixon, remembered him and offered to help produce a photo fit. She's coming in this afternoon."

"That's great news, well done."

"It wasn't my idea," said Alice.

"No, but you were brave enough to pursue it, so take some credit for that."

Alice didn't argue with Claire but she wasn't prepared to take any credit for it; she just wished she had thought of it first. It was bloody obvious and she was kicking herself that she hadn't.

"Listen Alice, you've been brilliant. I can't thank you enough for your help on this. Can you do me one more favour though? Can you send me a copy of the photo-fit when it's done?"

"No problem. We'll be going public with it anyway."

"That's great. Thanks again Alice," said Claire, who ended the call and made her way back to the incident room.

Claire sat down at her desk and started to process what she had just been told. *So the abductor clones Gallagher's plates and then Gallagher ends up in the river. Could Gallagher be the abductor, cloned his own plates and used another vehicle? No, that doesn't make any sense so what was the connection? It couldn't be a coincidence?* And then it struck her. *What if the mysterious earring belonged to Anne?*

"Claire, can I have a word?" asked DCI Miller.

Claire was so caught up in her thoughts that she hadn't even noticed the DCI enter the room.

"Claire, can we have a chat in my office, if you don't mind?" asked the DCI who immediately turned and headed back towards her office.

Claire followed her into the office and closed the door.

"There's been a development…wait, is that an engagement ring?" asked the DCI.

"Yes, Peter and I…"

"Congratulations, when did this happen?"

Claire hesitated and then decided to lie as that would be easier than trying to explain that it happened two nights ago but she chose not to wear the ring yesterday.

"Last night."

"That's great news. Did you pick the ring yourself?"

"No, Peter picked it." Claire was losing patience. "You said there had been a development?"

"Oh yes, you're never going to believe it but Maryhill have discovered that the cloned plates used on the van they were following on CCTV belonged to Donald Gallagher."

"Really," said Claire trying her best to act surprised. She was becoming good at it.

"Yes and they want to have a meeting to decide how best to take the case forward. Obviously, I'll share what we have on Gallagher's death with them and it's likely that they'll want to take the lead on it."

"I want to attend the meeting," said Claire grabbing the opportunity.

"Absolutely not; you are too close to it, Claire. We've already discussed this. I'll keep you informed."

"Yes, I know but what if the Lisa Chandler case is connected."

"What do you mean? You know that the only loose connection we had with Lisa's case was the earring and we now know it wasn't hers."

"Yes, but we also know that Gallagher's sister didn't recognise it so who does it belong to? What if it was my cousin's earring?"

DCI Miller was taken aback and suddenly realised that Claire could be right. "Okay, we'll need to check that out. I'll provide Maryhill with details of the earring. It's still their case, Claire," she said reinforcing her message.

Claire knew that any further protest would be futile. She had played all her cards and the DCI wouldn't budge. "Okay, but tell me you'll reconsider if the two cases are linked?"

"Let's just check that the earring belongs to your cousin first, before we do anything else. You were convinced that the earring belonged to Lisa Chandler not that long ago and were wrong about that! Remember?" said DCI Miller with a bit more venom in her tone.

Claire picked up the signal, nodded and left the room. When she got back to her office her mobile phone was ringing. It was her Mum.

"Hi Mum, what's up? What?" Oh my God, I'm on my way. Okay I'll be there as quick as I can."

Claire grabbed her coat and shouted across the room to Brian and the others. "Sorry but I'll need to go. My dad's had a heart attack and…"

Brian interrupted her. "That's terrible Claire, just go. I have everything under control here. I hope your dad is okay, now off you go. Oh, and I'll let the DCI know where you are."

"Thanks Brian," said Claire and ran out the door.

It took Claire almost 50 minutes to get to the hospital due to the traffic and a further 5 minutes to find a parking space. She immediately headed to Ward 1 and went to the nursing station where she was directed to the Intensive Care Unit. Claire saw her Mum as soon as she exited the elevator; she was sitting in a small waiting area all by herself.

"Hi Mum, where's Dad?" asked Claire looking around to see if there were any nurses or doctors around.

"He's still in intensive care. I've been waiting here for almost an hour now. They said that he'd suffered a minor heart attack and that his breathing is erratic. Apparently he's been put on a ventilator to help him breathe."

"But I thought he was on the mend when we spoke this morning," said Claire.

"I know and so did I. He tried to eat something, started coughing really badly, couldn't catch his breath and apparently that's what the doctor thinks triggered the heart attack."

"Poor Dad," said Claire thinking out loud. "But, at least he was in hospital when it happened. Goodness knows what would have happened if he'd been at home."

Claire's mum just nodded at the thought of it and physically shivered as the reality of what could have happened sunk in.

"Right, I'm going to find someone to give us an update," said Clare and strode off in search of a nurse. She eventually found one who was coming out of the ICU and was reassured that her father had stabilised and was going to be fine. Claire went back to her mum, told her the good news and suggested that she should go home and get some rest and something to eat. Claire would wait in the hospital until she got back.

Four hours later Barbara Redding returned to the hospital wearing a fresh set of clothes and was feeling much better. She had brought a few bits and pieces for her husband: toothbrush, pyjamas, slippers, etc., and was relieved to see that John had been moved back into his private room where Claire was sitting waiting.

"How is he doing Claire?" she asked.

"Much better Mum, his breathing has stabilised but he's still on oxygen. The doctor says they are going to keep him sedated until the infection has cleared."

"Thank God for that and thanks for being here with him love. Now you go off home and get a break. I'll stay here with your dad and let you know if anything changes."

"Are you going to stay overnight again?" asked Claire. "The doctor says there's no need as Dad will be sedated so it won't make any difference to him."

"Well, it will to me. I'll just worry more if I go home to an empty house."

Claire couldn't argue; she'd do the same if it was Peter lying there.

"Well okay. I'll come back after work to see how you both are."

"You're going back to work. Surely they can cope without you for one day?"

"We're in the middle of a big case and I'm beginning to think that my case and Anne's disappearance are linked. I really need to get back there but call me if anything happens."

"Do you really think both cases are linked?

"Well, we're waiting for confirmation from Maryhill, but yes, I believe they could be linked and if they are, I want to find Anne as soon as possible."

"Right then, well off you go. Don't let me hold you back."

Chapter Twenty - One

It was just after 5 pm when Claire arrived back at the office. The rush hour traffic had been horrendous and she was tired by the time she arrived back at the station. Brian was the only one left in the office and was sitting at his desk staring at his laptop. He saw Claire come in and immediately stood up to speak to her.

"How's your dad?" he asked.

"He's stable, it was a heart attack but he's okay. He's been sedated and my mum is with him. Hopefully we're over the worst. Any news here? Did Jim get an address for the missing lecturer?"

Brian shook his head. "Not a current address. He tried calling an old telephone number the university still had on record but got no answer. He's on his way to the Professor's old home address now to see if the current occupiers have a forwarding address. It's somewhere out in Gartocharn."

Claire nodded. "Anything else? What about the timeline that Billy was working on? Anything?"

Again Brian shook his head. "No nothing much to report. There's a copy of the timeline on the incident board if you want to take a look but nothing unusual jumped out at me. However, I have been promised the results from the DNA analysis this afternoon, which is why I'm still here."

"That's quick. I was thinking that would be tomorrow earliest," said Claire.

"Yes, well they agreed to prioritise our request. Apparently, it's just a case of comparing the DNA to existing DNA held on the data base. There are over 18 million different samples held on it worldwide, so I asked them to restrict it to Scotland only and they said that it would make a huge difference to the search time."

"Good thinking Brian, I'm glad one of us is on the ball."

Claire opened her laptop and signed in to check her emails. Her attention was immediately drawn to an email from DC McWilliams. This time, it was the photo-fit picture of the man in the pub. She had forgotten all about her earlier conversation with DC McWilliams. The man in the picture looked like a Neanderthal; big forehead, heavy eye brows, large square jaw. *It should be easy to recognise him,* thought Claire. She pondered how much information she should share with Brian and decided she could probably trust him. It was then that she also noticed an email from the DCI marked 'Earring 'in the subject heading. The DCI had heard back from Maryhill and now had confirmation that the ring found in Gallagher's procession belonged to Anne. At first Claire felt elated at the news but the latter part of the message was less easy to swallow. Maryhill were even more determined to take over the case as there were clear links between Anne and Gallagher, even though he was dead. The DCI also pointed out that Maryhill were currently searching for the vehicle which was registered to Gallagher as it was not parked outside his home.

Claire was furious and decided it was time Brian was brought up to speed with what she knew about her cousin's disappearance. However, before she could get a word in Brian was on his feet. "You're never going to believe this boss!"

"What now?" she said still fizzing from the DCI's email.

"I've got the DNA results back and they think the DNA shows traces of the Wallace clan?

"What, as in William Wallace – Braveheart?" asked Claire.

"Yes, the very same," said Brian.

"So how does that help us? Do we have to interview everybody in Dumbarton with the surname Wallace? she asked sarcastically.

"No boss, you're not getting it, are you?"

"No Brian, I'm not. I'm tired. I'm stressed and fucking raging at the DCI."

Her rant did not deter Brian from carrying on. "This DNA sample came from soil remember?"

"Yes, Brian I remember."

"And it was approximately 800 years old?"

"Yes, Brian…so what?"

"Well if you know your local history, and clearly you don't, you would know that William Wallace was held here in Dumbarton before being taken to London to be tortured and executed.

"And I don't suppose you know where he was held, do you?" she asked with even more sarcasm than before.

"I do and so does every school child born and raised in Dumbarton!" He paused a little, just enough to build up the tension. "He was held in Dumbarton Castle by Sir John Menteith, the Keeper of the Castle at the time, I think that was back in thirteen hundred and something so that would be approximately 800 years ago!"

"Keeper of the Castle?" asked Claire. "What's that all about?"

"Don't they teach you lot anything at university," said Brian grinning like the cat who got the cream. He'd wanted to use that particular line for some time now. It was only then that the penny finally dropped.

"Of course, and the traces of volcanic rock, it all makes sense now. Brian, you're a bloody genius. So, it's possible Lisa has been held somewhere in the grounds of the castle before being dumped in the river," said Claire.

"Right, so what are we waiting for, let's go there now and see what we can find." And then something else occurred to her. "Hold on, if Anne was taken by the same person as Lisa, then Anne could be held somewhere in the castle."

"Anne…your missing cousin, what's the connection?" asked Brian.

"Sorry, I was just about to tell you. It was Anne's earring that they found in Gallagher's jacket pocket and the number plates used on the van used for Anne's abduction belonged to Gallagher and Gallagher was a custodian of the castle."

"So he was!" said Brian. "Right, I'll need to get a hold of somebody from Historic Environment Scotland to meet us there; the castle will probably be closed at this time of night."

Brian made the call and eventually got a rather grumpy member of staff from the castle on the other end of the line. According to the Castle Attendant there was no way someone could be hidden in the castle without his knowledge.

Brian and Claire were waiting at the gates of the Castle when David Rooney, the grumpy Castle Attendant, arrived on the scene in his beaten up old jeep. He parked or more accurately abandoned his jeep outside the Rock Bowling Club. Rooney was approximately six feet five inches in height and looked like he could do with a good meal or six. He approached the gate without any word of a greeting and took out a large set of keys from his jacket pocket and proceeded to open the padlock and chains which were wrapped round both gates. He removed the heavy chain from one of the gates and then attached it to the other and then used the padlock to secure it. The wrought iron gates creaked and screeched as he pulled them open and then made his way up the dark staircase towards the Castle.

"Mind your step," he said to the two officers without looking back. "It can be really slippery when wet."

Both officers looked at each other and then followed Rooney up the stairs carefully looking down at the uneven steps the whole way up. By the time they reached the entrance to the Governor's House, Brian was gasping for a breath. He hated stairs and was grateful for the short delay while Rooney opened the two sets of doors leading to the house and then entered to turn off the alarm.

"You see. There's no way that anyone can get in here without me knowing about it?" he said pointedly.

"Does anyone else have access to the keys and the alarm?" asked Claire. She had pretty much ruled out Rooney as a suspect given he didn't match the physical description or photo-fit of the man in the pub but she was keeping an open mind at this stage, just in case Rooney was involved in some way or other.

"Yes, there are one or two others who look after the shop. And of course, the Keeper of the Castle has a set of keys but we never see him around here anymore. He'll probably show up when the Queen dies."

Claire was first to react. "What? What are you talking about?"

Rooney could see that Claire didn't know much about the history of the castle and started to do what he liked to do most in life; share his vast knowledge of the castle with anyone who was willing to listen. "Dumbarton Castle is one of three Royal Castles in Scotland. Tradition states that when the Sovereign dies, the Keeper of the Castle must present the keys to the new Sovereign so when Queen Elizabeth II dies we can expect a visit from the newly crowned King Charles, who will be presented with the keys by the Keeper of the Castle."

"That's fascinating," said Claire sarcastically. "So who is the Keeper of the Castle these days?"

"It's some General or other with a big fancy name. I've never met him but he must be in his eighties by now so I doubt if he's a suspect if that's what you're thinking. Anyway, enough of this chit-chat, where do you want to start?"

"We'll need to search every room, anywhere that someone could be held captive?"

"Right then, well that's the shop through there to the right. We can start there if you like and then we can move upstairs. There are a lot of rooms so this could take a while."

Chapter Twenty - Two

Anne was lying on her small bed thinking about the most recent conversation she'd had with Robert. It occurred to her that although she clearly hated being held captive, she realised that she was starting to look forward to her conversations with him. The boredom of being left alone in the cell on her own was far worse than being in his company and in fact their most recent conversations about religion and philosophy were really interesting. He was clearly well educated and despite looking like a creature from the bronze-age he was actually quite mannerly and well spoken. She had also come to the conclusion that he was clearly carrying out some form of research and using her as a human Guinea Pig but she couldn't quite work out what he was up to. She decided she was going to confront him and ask what it was he was doing or trying to achieve by keeping her and asking all these questions. *Perhaps, she could help him if she knew what he actually wanted?*

Robert entered the room carrying a tray with two small plates of food. "Do you mind if I join you for dinner tonight?" he asked.

This was a first and Anne nodded her head in agreement.

He closed the door and passed her one of the plates which had the knife and fork balanced on the edge but managed to drop the knife which landed on the dirty floor. "Never mind you can use mine," he said and passed the clean knife over to Anne and then turned around and bent down to pick up the other knife.

In an instant Anne saw her opportunity and stabbed him in the middle of the back with the knife. Robert screamed in agony and fell towards the floor writhing in pain, twisting and turning trying to get a hold of the knife. Anne leapt over him, made it to the door and pulled it wide open. She stepped out into the small narrow corridor. Looked left, then right, felt cold air coming from the right and ran as fast as she could. She stopped at the end of the corridor and looked back only to see Robert rushing towards her with the blood covered knife in his hand. She found the ladder and started climbing as fast as she could towards the cold air which was rushing in from what looked like an old drain cover above. She reached the top of the ladder and pushed against the heavy iron cover but it didn't move. She screamed as loud as she could, praying that someone could hear her but no one could. It was then that she felt Robert's powerful hand grip her ankle and slowly pull her down the ladder towards him. He put the knife in his pocket to free up his other hand and then dragged Anne, screaming and kicking, all the way back along the corridor and pushed her inside the cell. Anne heard the door slam shut and the three bolts being slid back into place. Her heart sank.

Claire, Brian and Rooney had reached the top floor of the castle and had found nothing.

"I don't suppose there are any hidden passageways or tunnels?" asked Brian clutching at straws.

"Not that I'm aware of," said Rooney. "I did try to tell you but you didn't listen."

"What about other parts of the castle?" asked Claire. "I mean, this is just the house, are there any other buildings where someone could be hidden in the grounds of the castle?"

"Well there's the French Prison at the very top of the castle but I doubt if you'll find anything up there; they are opened to the public so not ideal if you want to hide someone," he said snidely.

"I suppose we better go and take a look," said Brian, who was not looking forward to climbing even more stairs.

Rooney led the two officers back down to the entrance to the house, turning off lights as he went. He closed and locked all doors and turned the alarm back on before heading up the outer stairs leading up to the French Prison. Having inspected all the cells in the prison and having found nothing, they came back outside and headed down the stairs back towards the Governor's house. Before making their way down to the stairs which led to the road below, Claire stopped and turned around to take another look at the castle's grounds. It really was too dark to make out any detail and probably too dangerous to go searching around the rest of the place in the dark.

"Are you sure that there's nowhere else here that a person could be hidden?" she asked Rooney again.

He shook his head. "I know it's none of my business but why do you think someone is using the castle as a hiding place?" asked Rooney. "I mean, what brought you here?"

Claire was reluctant to share any details with Rooney as she still didn't fully trust him so she ignored his question and asked another."

"Is it true that William Wallace was held here before he was sent to England to be killed?"

"Well, we know that he was held by Menteith before being handed over to the English and that Menteith was based here in the castle at that time. Why do you ask?"

Claire ignored the question again and asked another. "So, if you were Menteith, where would you hold your prisoners?"

"In the cells below the castle would be my best guess?" said Rooney.

"But you didn't show us any cells under the castle."

"Not this castle," he looked at the young DI with contempt. "I'm referring to the medieval castle which would have been occupied by Menteith in the thirteen hundreds and was destroyed many years ago. The Governor's House is actually Georgian!"

Claire gave Brian a withering look and he just shrugged his shoulders in response. How was he supposed to know that the original castle had been destroyed!

Claire turned suddenly. "What was that?"

"What?" said Rooney and Brian, almost simultaneously.

"Didn't you hear it? It sounded like metal scraping something?"

"Probably noise from the road below," said Rooney.

"No, it came from behind me, I'm sure of it," she said and turned back towards the grounds of the castle. She stared into the darkness again and then she thought she saw some movement in the shadows.

"It'll be the wind playing tricks…."

"Stop, Police!" shouted Claire and immediately ran back up the stairs. Brian turned to Rooney and shouted. "Wait for us down at your car. Do not leave here, understand?" Brian then ran up the stairs in pursuit of Claire.

Rooney was still in shock. He nodded, turned and started down the stairs so quickly that he almost fell.

When Brian made it to the top of the stairs he couldn't see Claire or the person she was chasing. He bent down sucking the cold night air into his over worked lungs. "Claire," he shouted as loud as he could.

Silence, he waited for a few seconds but there was no response.

He went further round the back of the Governor's house and shouted again.

"Over here," she shouted back.

He could barely hear her voice but it was enough to give him the general direction. He ran as fast as he could towards the sound and headed around the other side of the Governor's House where he spotted her and the man she had been chasing. She had forced him onto some scaffolding which had been built on the far side of the castle to allow further renovation to the outside of the castle walls. Brian approached them slowly, making sure that he blocked off the only escape route the man had, other than jumping off the scaffolding to the ground over 60 feet below. When Brian got closer he could hear Claire trying to talk the man down.

Claire had recognised him as soon as she had got close enough. It was the same man in the photo-fit that DC McWilliams had sent her and therefore she knew that Anne must be somewhere nearby and was keen to reason with him. *Get Anne to safety first and then sort out the rest,* she thought.

The man spotted Brian approaching the scaffold and pulled out the knife from his pocket. Both officers froze at the sight of the weapon. This changed the whole situation.

Claire, who was still on the scaffolding started to move away from the edge where she was standing. "Okay, let's not make this situation any worse! Put the knife down," she said, as she slowly shuffled herself towards Brian who was now standing on the double planks of wood which served as a bridge from the parapet to the outer scaffolding.

The man started to approach Claire. "Back off and you won't get hurt!" he said.

"That's not going to happen so put the knife down," said Brian who moved nearer.

"Back off!" Robert shouted, waiving the knife around in a threatening manner.

"Where is she? Where is Anne?" asked Claire.

The revelation that Claire knew about Anne appeared to startle the man and Brian took the opportunity to lunge for the knife. Robert caught sight of Brian's movement from the corner of his eye and instinctively swung round to block him with the knife still in his hand. The blow caught Brian on the right hand side of his waist and the knife went in deep. Brian dropped forward on his knees, his hands holding the wound which was now oozing warm blood through his fingers. He looked at Claire briefly before collapsing with the pain.

"Brian!" shouted Claire.

"I…I didn't mean it. You saw it, he attacked me. It was an accident," said the man, still holding the knife in his hand.

Claire went cold and then all her rage, all her anger exploded as she ran, jumped and karate kicked the man full on the chest and despite his clear weight advantage, he lost balance and fell backwards, the back of his legs hit the low metal railing and because he was top heavy the weight of his upper body pulled him backwards over the edge. Claire's forward momentum almost took her off the edge of the scaffold but she managed to turn her body in time to grab hold of the railing and then pull herself back up onto the scaffold floor. She immediately went to Brian and managed to turn him over to see his wound. It looked bad and there was a fair amount of blood leaking from the wound. She took off the small headscarf she was wearing and pushed it into the wound as hard as she could. Brian winced with the pain of the pressure but knew it was necessary to reduce the flow of the blood.

"Hang in there Brian, you're going to be alright," said Claire, praying that she was right.

Brian looked at her unable to respond due to the pain but clearly hearing her and communicated this through his eyes.

Rooney, who had been watching all the action from the road below and had seen the man fall, had made his way back up to the castle. Claire saw him approach and called him over. "He's been stabbed. Press down hard on this scarf to stop the bleeding and keep the pressure on it. I'll get an ambulance."

Rooney was in a total daze and did what he was told without reply.

"Hello, control, this is DI Redding. I'm at Dumbarton Castle and need an ambulance right away. DS O'Neill has been stabbed and another man, the perpetrator has fallen from some scaffolding. No, I don't know his condition."

"Claire looked down to see the man lying spread-eagled on the grass bank below.

"He's not moving but I don't know if he's unconscious or dead. I'll go down and check." She turned and looked at Rooney. "You stay here, keep the pressure on that wound and shout down for me if his condition gets worse. I'm going down to see if that bastard is still alive."

Rooney had discovered a new level of respect for the young detective and was now happy to do whatever she instructed.

Claire ran down the steps to the castle gates and then ran up the grass bank to where the man was lying, arms and legs splayed out like a broken Swastica. She put her ear to his mouth to check for breathing and could sense a very feint whisper of air. She picked up her phone. "Hello, control, yes he's still alive but his breathing is very weak. He's unconscious and has blood coming from the back of his head. Yes, we need two ambulances. Okay, thanks, now can you put me through to DCI Miller?"

The phone clicked twice and connected to DCI Miller who unsurprisingly was shocked to hear the recent turn of events. Claire quickly explained to the DCI what had happened and requested police dogs to search the castle grounds for Anne. The DCI agreed to get them there as soon as possible but in the meantime the priority was to get DS O'Neill to hospital. The DCI told Claire that she would meet her at the castle as soon as she could.

Claire hung up and could hear what she thought was an ambulance approaching in the distance. It wasn't an ambulance, it was a paramedic. Thankfully, it had been stationed just off the Lomond Gate roundabout and was only five minutes away. The ambulances which were based in the Vale of Leven Hospital would take slightly longer to get there. Claire ran down to meet the paramedic who stopped the vehicle just outside the castle gates. As soon as the paramedic got out the vehicle Claire directed him to attend to DS O'Neill, who had a stab wound and was bleeding badly. The paramedic wanted to check on the man who had fallen first but Claire insisted priority was given to her colleague. The paramedic followed the instructions and ran up to the castle to attend to Brian. Claire ran up the bank again to where the kidnapper was lying. He had come round and was groaning with the pain. She knelt down beside him. "Where is she? Where is Anne Duncan?" she asked.

He looked at Claire with bemusement. How did she know? How did she find him? He had completely underestimated the local Police and now it was over. He would never finish his research; it was all he lived for and now it was over. He tried to speak to the young detective and Claire lowered her head towards his mouth to hear him.

"My research, she's ...." He said and then nothing. His breathing had stopped.

"Oh no," said Claire. "Wake up, come on, don't you dare die on me," she said and shook him hard but there was no response. She had no choice but to administer CPR. She tilted his head back to ensure his airways were clear and pinched his nose and then blew air into his lungs twice and then started chest compressions in time with 'Staying Alive', just as she had been trained to do. After 30 compressions, she blew more air in his mouth and started again. She was beginning to tire when the first ambulance arrived. *Thank God for that*, she thought and shouted down to the ambulance driver.

"Up here quick, he's stopped breathing," shouted Claire. "You'll need a defibrillator."

The ambulance driver acknowledged DI Redding by waving and instructed his colleague to get the 'de-fib' out the back of the ambulance. Claire stood back as they approached and watched as they quickly cut open the man's clothing and stuck the two electronic pads on the man's chest.

"Clear," the ambulance driver shouted as he pressed the button and shocked the man. Nothing. "Clear," he shouted as he tried again, and this time they got a reading.

"What happened to him?" asked one of the men.

"He fell from up there," said Claire and pointed all the way up to the top level of scaffolding directly above their heads. She couldn't be bothered trying to explain what actually happened. This was not the time or place for that. The second ambulance arrived and this time Claire ran down to meet it. She immediately explained that the paramedic was attending to her police colleague up in the castle and directed them up to where Brian was still lying on the ground. They grabbed a portable stretcher which looked like it was made out of some form of lightweight fibre glass and followed DI Redding up the stairs. Claire looked at the flimsy looking board and thought to herself, *you might need something a bit stronger than that to lift Brian!*

As Claire approached the scaffolding, she could see the paramedic had removed Brian's shirt and had packed and bandaged the wound. Rooney was standing further back and still appeared to be in shock.

"Is he going to be alright?" she asked the paramedic.

"Yes, but he has lost a lot of blood so we'll need to get a fluid drip into him as soon as possible but yes, he'll live."

"Claire," said Brian faintly. Did you get him?"

Claire was relieved to hear his voice and almost burst into tears.

"Yes Brian, I got him" she replied and bent down and took his hand.

"And Anne?" he said.

"Not yet, but we will. I've asked for police dogs so I'm sure we'll find her if she's here."

Just then the lead ambulance officer stepped forward and asked Claire to stand aside. The two men carefully rolled Brian one way, slid half a board under him and then turned him onto the other side and slid the other half of the board and clicked the two halves together. The paramedic had given him some morphine to dull the pain so he didn't mind being moved around so much.   The two ambulance men then strapped Brian onto the board and carefully lifted him up and slowly made their way down towards the ambulance. The paramedic walked beside Brian keeping an eye on the wound and the bandaging. Claire and Rooney followed them down the stairs.

Claire saw that the other two ambulance men had started to put Robert onto a stretcher and ran up to them to check on his progress.

"Is he going to make it?" she asked.

"We managed to get a pulse but it's very weak. Can you ask the paramedic to help us? We need someone to hold the oxygen supply until we get him into the ambulance."

Claire went down and spoke to the paramedic who immediately left Brian and headed up the grass bank to assist the other two. She followed the paramedic up the bank and could see the man had been turned on his side to get the stretcher board underneath but instead of putting him back down, the ambulance officer was looking at his back.

"What's up?" asked Claire.

"There appears to be a nasty wound on his back. It looks like he must have hit a sharp object when he fell but I don't see anything around here which could have caused that."

Claire looked around scanning the ground for anything sharp. "He was holding a knife when he fell. That's what he stabbed my colleague with, up there," she said pointing to the scaffold tower above their heads.

"Well I don't see it lying around but I suppose it could have landed anywhere."

Claire was suddenly concerned that they appeared to have lost a key piece of evidence. The two ambulance men assisted by the paramedic lifted the stretcher and headed down to the second ambulance.

"Hold on a minute, said Claire. She approached the stretcher and started to search the man's pockets. She was hoping to find some form of identification but all he had was a set of keys, which she put in her coat pocket. "Right on you go."

Chapter Twenty - Three

The first ambulance started to make its way back towards the hospital and passed the DCI who had just arrived in a squad car followed by a van full of uniformed Police Officers.

Claire met the DCI at her car but before giving her an update she instructed the police officers to start searching the castle grounds for Anne.

"Thank God Brian's going to be alright," said the DCI.

Claire nodded. "We really need those dogs as soon as possible; it's really dark up there and Mr Rooney here is not aware of anywhere else a person could be hidden. Are you Mr Rooney?" asked Claire.

Rooney approached the DCI. "That's correct, we have searched all the buildings that I know about. Is it okay if I leave now?"

Claire spoke before the DCI could respond. "Sorry, but we'll need you to give a full statement Mr Rooney. After all you did witness the whole incident from down here, didn't you?" she said, and looked up to the scaffolding. A chill ran down her spine as she relived the moment when Brian was stabbed with the knife.

"Yes, well I saw you kick the man in the chest and saw him fall if that's what you mean?" he asked.

"Yes, but you must have seen the man stab my colleague with a knife before I kicked him?" said Claire.

"No, I didn't see any knife," said Rooney.

Claire looked back up to the scaffolding and then realised. "Of course, he was holding the knife in his right hand and was side on to you. There's no way you would have seen the knife from this angle."

"Never mind," said the DCI. "We have the knife which will have his finger prints all over it so…"

"Sorry Ma'am but the knife seems to have gone missing when he fell over the edge."

"When you kicked him over the edge," said Rooney correcting the DI.

If looks could kill then Rooney was a dead man standing.

"Okay Mr Rooney, you'll get your chance to give your statement. Why don't you go over to my car and keep warm while we search for the missing girl," said the DCI pointing over to her vehicle.

Rooney looked at Claire and then hastily went and sat in the DCI's squad car.

Claire turned to the DCI. "There was a knife. How else could he have stabbed Brian," she said defensively.

"So, you kicked him over the edge of the scaffolding?" asked the DCI drawing in a deep breath.

"It was self defence. He was coming at me with the knife. I didn't mean for him to fall. I wanted him alive to tell us where he had hidden Anne. I gave him bloody CPR down here trying to him keep alive!" she exclaimed.

DCI Miller nodded, giving Claire the benefit of the doubt. "Okay, I dare say we'll find the knife. I'll get one of our guys to search the area with a metal detector. It's bound to turn up. In the meantime, you stay clear of that area. I don't want there to be any suggestion of us tampering with evidence. Understood?"

"Yes, Ma'am," said Claire biting her tongue.

"Oh, and Claire, I've asked Maryhill to send someone over with an item of clothing belonging to your cousin, you know, to give the dogs her scent."

"Good thinking Ma'am. I should have thought of that! I wish those bloody dogs would hurry up and get here though," said Claire. Her adrenalin had worn off now and she was beginning to shiver physically with cold.

"Go wait in the van and warm up. I'll go up and see how uniform are getting on with the search," said DCI Miller, who turned and headed up the stairs.

Claire headed towards the car where Rooney was sitting. She was about to give him an earful but thought better off it and climbed into the police van, which was parked directly behind the DCI's BMW.

As Claire sat there in quietness, a thought suddenly occurred to her. The man's knife looked as if it already had blood on it before he stabbed Brian. What if he had attacked Anne before she heard him move about? Her heart started to race. If that was the case Anne could be lying bleeding to death somewhere up there. *Where are those fucking dogs!*

Another squad car arrived at the castle and Anne immediately jumped out the van to meet it. She recognised the driver instantly. It was Alice McWilliams. She had been sent to collect the item of clothing and was holding a woollen hat in a clear plastic bag. She got out the car and handed the bag over to Claire.

"Hi Claire, fancy meeting you here," she said knowingly. "This is your cousin's hat. Your Aunt says that Anne has been wearing it all winter and it's not been washed yet so should be good enough for the dogs to get her scent." DC Williams looked around her. "Are they not here yet?"

"Not yet, apparently they're on their way though," said Claire.

"So, do you think you have him then" asked Alice.

"Yes, well he certainly fits the photo-fit of the man in the pub. Any luck with identifying him?"

"Not yet. There was no match on the database," said Alice.

"Didn't think we would get that lucky," said Claire. She put her hands in her coat pockets and suddenly remembered the keys and took them out. "These are his keys. While we are waiting for the dogs, let's see if his vehicle is nearby?" said Claire and marched over the car park and started pressing the electronic key fob in search of flashing indicators. They made their way round the side of the castle and noticed a white van sitting on it's own in an unlit parking bay. As soon as Claire got close enough she pressed the button and like magic the lights flashed and the doors opened. Claire put on a pair of latex gloves, which she always kept in her pocket, and took a quick look around inside the vehicle's cabin. She then opened the rear door. The large boot space was empty but was clearly big enough to take a body if required. "Right, we'll need to get forensics down here to check this vehicle out. There's nothing obvious but you never know what they'll find. Can you call in the number plate and see if we can identify him that way."

"There's no need," said Alice. "I know who the van belongs to."

Claire looked at Alice and then she knew. "Donald Gallagher?"

"The very same," said Alice beaming with pleasure.

"So, the Neanderthal must have killed Gallagher, as well as Lisa."

"Neanderthal?" asked Alice.

"Sorry that's just how I think of him. I wish I knew his bloody name!"

Alice smiled and nodded and then noticed a police van coming down Castle Road. "Here comes the dogs," she said.

"Not before time!" said Claire. "Come on, let's go and find my cousin."

Chapter Twenty – Four

It didn't take Claire very long to brief the dog handlers who took the hat and let both dogs get a good whiff of Anne's scent. Claire led them up to the area where she first caught sight of the suspect and very quickly the dogs starting sniffing the ground and then moving round in ever increasing circles until one of the dogs got something and started to pull its handler towards the far corner of the castle and then it stopped.

Claire followed the dog handler but still couldn't see anywhere obvious that Anne could be hidden.

"Down there," shouted the dog handler and shone his torch on what appeared to be a metal drain cover, which was camouflaged by the shrubbery, which had been placed over it.

Claire tried to lift it but it was far too heavy. She called over a couple of officers who together managed to lift an edge and slide it across the ground. Claire recognised the sound it made. This was it. This was his hiding place. She carefully climbed down the ladder, followed by one of the officers who helped lift the cover, and headed along the dark corridor but had to stop as it was too dark. She took out her phone and turned on the flash light. "Anne, are you here?" she shouted.

Anne was cowering at the back of her room, too terrified to move, still in shock from her earlier encounter with Robert. At first, she thought she had imagined hearing the voice but when Claire called out a second time, she jumped to her feet and started shouting back. "In here, I'm in here!" She banged the door as hard as she could and Claire immediately knew where she was being held. Anne could hear the bolts being slid opened and was really surprised when Claire finally pushed the large door open.

"Anne, thank God. Are you alright? Are you hurt?" she asked looking her cousin up and down; checking for knife wounds.

"Where's Robert? Did you get him?" she asked, looking over Claire's shoulder and got a fright when the other officer appeared

"It's okay Anne. I got him. Robert, was that his name?" asked Claire.

"That's what he told me but I think he made it up," said Anne who took a step forward and almost collapsed into Claire's arms.

"Right, just sit there on the bed for a minute." She turned to the police officer behind her. Call in the paramedic. I want her checked out before we get her up the ladder. And tell him to wear gloves. We need to preserve the crime scene as much as possible for SOC when they get here.

The paramedic arrived and carefully climbed down the ladder wearing gloves as instructed. Claire left the paramedic to check Anne and went back down the corridor and opened the other door which led to a small room. Claire could hear the sound of what she thought must be a small generator coming from the back of the room and could see the two small TV monitors with images of Anne's room. Claire pulled a pair of latex gloves from her coat pocket and put them on before carefully looking through the hand written notes that had been left lying on the desk. The more Claire read, the more she understood about what Anne's captor was doing. After a few minutes had passed, she heard the paramedic and Anne walk past the doorway and decided that she had seen enough and followed them back along the dank corridor towards the ladder. Anne looked much steadier on her feet than before and Claire was impressed by how easily she managed to climb the ladder on her own steam. When Anne climbed out of the drain she was startled to see lots of police officers, moving around busy doing their work, scouring the area for evidence. DCI Miller approached Anne who was clearly disorientated.

"Hello, Anne, I'm DCI Miller, it's really good to meet you. You can thank your cousin for all this. She was the one who led us to the castle and found you," she said, looking down at the drain as Claire appeared.

"It wasn't just me. In fact, if anyone should be thanked it should be DC O'Neill. It was his local knowledge that connected the dots," said Claire.

Anne turned to her big cousin and hugged her. "Thank you Claire. I can't believe I didn't say that down there." She was now in tears and Claire was soon to follow. The DCI stood back as the two cousins embraced each other.

"Where is DS O'Neill, I would like to thank him in person," said Anne looking around the scene.

"He's on his way to hospital. He was stabbed trying to stop Robert escaping. He'll be alright though."

"And Robert?" Anne asked.

Claire looked at the DCI unsure as to how much information they should share with Anne.

"He's also on his way to hospital. Let's just say he had a bad fall?" said the DCI.

"What about the stab wound?" Anne asked. "I stabbed him with a knife just before you rescued me."

Claire responded. "So that's why he suddenly appeared out of nowhere. He must have needed some attention as he couldn't treat the wound on his back himself." She could see that the DCI was confused and so she went onto explain. "The ambulance officer spotted that his back was bleeding but we put it down to the fall. We really do need to find that knife though?"

"Yes, but at least we now have independent corroboration that there was a knife, presumably the same one Anne used on him," said DCI Miller.

Claire nodded. "Well done Anne, if you hadn't stabbed him we might never have found you."

The paramedic who had been waiting patiently to the side stepped forward. "I think we should get Anne into hospital to get fully checked before any more questioning."

DCI Miller nodded in agreement and the paramedic led Anne carefully down toward his emergency vehicle. Claire followed them down to where the vehicle was parked and told Anne that she would tell her Mum and Dad that she was safe and was just going to the hospital as a precaution. Anne thanked Claire again and waved from the vehicle as it made its way to the nearest hospital in the Vale of Leven.

From where she was standing Claire could see one of the police officers with a metal detector searching the embankment for the missing knife. She was less concerned now that Anne had confirmed there had been a knife and was sure it would turn up.

She immediately phoned her Aunt Cathy to give her the good news and then called her Mum.

"Hi Mum, we've found Anne," said Claire.

"Oh Claire, that's fantastic news. Is she okay?"

"Yes, but clearly she is still in shock but she's safe and well and is on her way to the Vale of Leven Hospital for a full check-up."

"Oh that's such a relief. Your Aunt Cathy must have been over the moon with the news!"

"She was, Mum, so how's Dad doing?"

"Oh, he's doing okay but they put him into isolation and told me to stay at home."

"What? Why?"

"Apparently they think he's got something called Coronavirus!"

"Coronavirus. What's that?" asked Claire.

"Haven't you been watching the news?"

"Mum, when do I ever have time to watch the news?"

"Well apparently it started in China and it's making its way through Europe."

"Really and how bad is it?" asked Claire.

"It's pretty bad. Lots of people have died in China."

"Well let's hope Dad doesn't have it. When will they know for sure?"

"They've had to send samples away to somewhere in England to get tested but they think he has all the symptoms; bad cough, temperature, headaches and so on. Oh, and they said you should isolate too since you've been in contact with him."

"What? That's ridiculous. Anyway, he was wearing an oxygen mask the whole time I saw him so there's no way I could have caught it."

"Well, that's what they said. They also said that the government is considering some kind of lockdown."

"Lockdown? What does that mean?" she asked, her voice reaching a higher octave with every question.

"I don't really know but that's what they are saying love."

"Okay Mum. I suppose we'll just need to wait and see. Poor old Dad, stuck in a hospital all on his own with no one to talk to."

"I know. Anyway that's great news about Anne. I'll need to get on the phone to your Aunt Cathy. She'll be so pleased. Bye love."

"Bye Mum." said Claire.

Claire hung up the phone and could see that the SOC team had arrived while she was on the phone. She directed them up to where the DCI was standing and explained that, in addition to anything else that they found there, she wanted them to collect a sample of the soil around the doorway to the cell. It was essential they could match this soil with the sample found under Lisa Chandler's nails. Claire was determined to give some form of closure and explanation to Lisa's parents and this would be confirmation. She also asked them to check out the white van parked on the far side of the castle and handed over the keys to the lead SOCO.

Claire headed back up to where the DCI was standing.

"Bad news Claire," said the DCI.

"Oh no, not Brian!"

"No, sorry, not Brian, Brian is fine but I've just heard that Anne's kidnapper died before they could get him into hospital."

"What? Oh shit!" said Claire.

"Oh shit indeed. There will need to be an enquiry into his death!"

"An enquiry?"

"Yes, which means you can't be involved with the remainder of the investigation!"

"But I found him and I stopped him from harming anyone else!" pleaded Claire.

"I know and I want you to know that I intend to commend you and Brian for outstanding police work and bravery! Now, it's getting late and the SOC Team is going to be here for some time. Why don't you go home to that fiancé of yours and celebrate getting your cousin back home safely."

"Thanks Ma'am, I'll do that."

Fiancé! She still wasn't used to being engaged and worse still, she and Peter had still to have that little chat about having a family. She was absolutely dreading it!

Claire headed down to her car to where DC McWilliams was waiting for her.

"I'm off the case," she said before the DC could speak.

"What? Why?

"The bugger who stabbed Brian died in the ambulance so there will need to be a police enquiry into his death."

"Oh shit!" said Alice looking more concerned than Claire was feeling.

"It'll be fine," said Claire. "Anyway you looked like you were going to tell me something."

"Oh, yes, I thought I would check out the vehicle and ran the chassis number through the system; just to be sure that it was Donald Gallagher's van and guess what?"

Claire was in no mood for guessing games. "What?" she asked rather sharply.

"It belongs to someone called William Fairbairn-Smythe."

Claire immediately recognised the name. "That would be Professor William Fairbairn-Smythe."

Alice was stunned. "Don't tell me you know of him?"

"Not really, but he was a person of interest in the Lisa Chandler case. It looks like we were on the right tracks though and probably would have caught up with him eventually. You should go and let my DCI know that you've identified him or at least his van. Well done Alice."

Chapter Twenty - Five

When Claire arrived home Peter appeared to be in a good mood and was clearly relieved to hear that her cousin had been found. However, his mood changed when Claire told him that she was now subject to a Police enquiry.

"That seems really unfair Claire. You solve the case, stop the bad guy and you are the one under investigation!" he said indignantly.

"I know but it's just procedure and I did kill him or at least caused his death. The DCI actually said she was going to commend me for excellent police work."

"Well, at least she's got your back, or so it appears! And you said they didn't find the knife. How's that possible?"

"Well, they might have found it by now. The SOC team know what they're looking for so it's only a matter of time and anyway, Anne and Brian will back me up so it will be okay."

"Just doesn't seem right that's all. Anyway enough chat about work. How's your Dad doing?"

"Oh, sorry, I should have told you. Have you heard about this Coronavirus thing?"

"Who hasn't, it's been all over the news. He doesn't have that, does he? It can be really bad, or so they say," said Peter looking really concerned.

So much so that Claire was starting to worry that she might have been a bit dismissive of her mother earlier on. Her mum could be a bit melodramatic at times.

"They're sending some samples away for tests but he seems to be doing better now, albeit he's been isolated."

"Oh really!"

"Yes, and so has my mum."

"And what about you? You were with your Dad for a while. Have you to isolate?"

"No chance. The doctor did suggest it but Dad was wearing a mask the whole time I was with him so I shouldn't really be at risk. Apparently it's an airborne virus or something like that," said Claire. She stood up and went over to the cooker.

"How about I make dinner for a change or maybe we should go out and properly celebrate our engagement!" she suggested, desperately trying to change the subject.

"I don't think we should go out, not if you could be carrying the virus, anyway it's a bit late and, well..." He paused before completing the sentence.

"I've been meaning to talk to you about us and the whole issue of having a family together. I've been giving it some thought."

Claire's heart sank. "Oh, right!" she said.

"Yes, I have a proposal?"

"Another one?" she joked trying to lighten the mood.

Peter picked up her poor attempt at humour and smiled. "Yes, another one."

He picked up the half full bottle of red wine which was sitting on the table and then grabbed two wine glasses from the cupboard. "Come on let's go through to the living room and have a seat. You can come too Sally, come on."

Sally and Claire followed Peter into the small living room. Peter poured two large glasses of wine and they sat down. Sally sat up beside Peter as usual so Claire sat opposite him.

"So, here's what I've been thinking," said Peter.

"I think I understand where you are coming from, not wanting to have a family and…"

"It's not that…" Claire started to say but Peter stopped her.

"Just hear me out first and then you can have your say. I know how much you love your job and can see why you feel that having a family wouldn't be the right thing to do. So, what if I can assure you that having a family would not get in the way of your work. He continued before she could interrupt. "Now, I know you would need time off to have the baby and so on but what if I was to give up work and look after the wee one and let you get back to work as soon as you were fit enough?"

Claire was speechless at first. This was not what she was expecting at all. "I, eh, I don't know what to say. Could we afford that? You know, to live on one wage? It sounds good but would it really work?"

"We will make it work and don't worry about the money, I've got some savings put away which should get us by for a few years," he said before she could respond. *And if that runs out I can always resurrect my old business,* he thought to himself.

"You really are willing to give up your work to have a family? It means that much to you?"

"More than willing and yes, it means that much to me!" said Peter, who meant every word of it. All his life he had longed for a stable family environment; something he had been denied as a child. "So, what do you think?" he asked, eager to hear her response now that he had said his piece.

There was a deftly silence.

"Claire?" he prompted.

Claire was in tears. "Well it certainly sounds like it could work. Can you let me think about it a bit more before I commit to anything?"

"Of course, take as long you need," said Peter standing up inviting her to come and hug him. "I've also been thinking about the wedding. We don't need to have a big fancy wedding if you really don't want one."

"I really don't," said Claire.

Chapter Twenty – Six

Claire entered the surgical recovery ward in the Royal Alexandria Hospital in Paisley, where she could see Brian, who was lying in the small bed, sitting partly upright, looking very bored.

"Hi Brian, how are you?" she asked and sat down beside him.

Brian's mood immediately changed when he saw Claire approach the bed.

"Oh hi Claire, it's so good to see you. Honestly, the boredom is killing me. I really need to get out of here before I go stir crazy."

"When do you think they'll let you out?"

"Well, the doctor says the wound is healing nicely; there's no internal damage other than my kidney being nicked by the knife but they stitched that up and said it should heal very quickly. It'll be another couple of days as long as there's no infection," he said, clearly frustrated.

Claire looked around the small room with three other beds; no private room for Brian. "Are you getting any sleep? Can't be easy with all this noise around you?" she asked.

"It's not as bad at night when the lights go out but some of these poor souls have dementia and are waiting for beds in nursing homes. They shouldn't really be here but there's nowhere else for them to go until a place becomes available. I never realised it was so bad until I came here. Anyway, enough of that, tell me about the case. What's happening, did you identify the bugger?"

"Yes, we did. His name was William Fairbairn-Smythe." Claire waited for his reaction.

"You're kidding. The missing professor we were looking for?" asked Brian.

"The very same," said Claire.

"So is that how he knew both the girls then?" he asked, as he began to process this new piece of information. "Did he teach them both?"

"No, not both of them, just Lisa but Anne did attend the university so the DCI thinks he might have spotted her there."

"Right, but why did he kidnap them? What was his motive? He must have some reason other than he knew them both at university?"

Claire nodded. "I managed to read some of his paperwork before I was taken off the case and…"

"Wait a minute. You're off the case?"

Claire explained all about the need for an enquiry but was keen to continue with her theory on what the professor was up to and then she remembered another wee piece of information that she knew Brian would love to hear.

"Remember, that big numpty Rooney," she said.

"How could I forget him?" said Brian. "Although, to be fair, he did help stop my wound from bleeding while you were sorting out the professor."

"True. Anyway, at one point he said that the Keeper of the Castle was a General with some big fancy name, or words to that effect."

"Yeah, I remember."

"Well it turns out Professor William Fairbairn-Smythe was his son and that's how he had the keys to the castle. And we now think that's how he knew about the hidden cells. According to his father, William would spend almost all of the summer holidays playing in the castle while his Dad had meetings with the other custodians of the castle including, guess who?"

"Who?" asked Brian.

"Donald Gallagher. I reckon Gallagher must have stumbled across the Professor and because he knew Gallagher would recognise him, he had to rid of Gallagher. Let's face it, who could forget that face?" said Claire.

"Well all that makes sense but it doesn't explain what the hell the Professor was up to. Why kidnap the girls? What did he want with them?"

"We'll never really know but from what I read and from what Anne said about her time with him I think I could have a good guess."

"Come on then Claire. Don't keep me in suspense," pleaded Brian, now desperate to hear her theory.

"Okay, so when I was down in the cells with Anne, I had a quick look at some of the papers lying about in the Professor's makeshift office. From what I could tell he was obsessed with a guy called Fairbairn who published a well-known theory referred to as 'Fairbairn's Object Relations Theory of attachment to the Abuser'.

"Never heard of it," said Brian.

"Well according to Fairbairn, his theory explained why some children who had been abused by their parents were surprisingly attached to their abusive parents, and in some cases more so than those children who had not been abused."

"Right, but that doesn't explain what the Professor was up to, does it," said Brian, who was now totally confused.

"No, it doesn't, but have you heard of the Stockholm syndrome?" asked Claire.

"I think so. Is that the one about hostages developing some kind of relationship or bond with their kidnappers?"

"Yes, but did you know that the Stockholm syndrome is not recognised by most psychologists even though the FBI say that 5% of hostage victims show signs of the syndrome. To be honest I had to look that bit up."

"Well that's all very interesting Claire but I still don't get what our Professor was up to," said Brian.

"Well the reason why it was not accepted was because most psychologists think that it can be explained by Fairbairn's theory except it refers to adults and the abuse takes the form of being denied your freedom, as in a hostage situation. Well, it appears our Professor had a different theory which he was desperately trying to prove." Claire paused for dramatic effect.

"Come on Claire, don't leave me hanging!" said Brian

"Well, I think he was trying to prove that the opposite was the case with adults. Instead of abusing his hostages, he cared for them and tried to form a relationship of trust and understanding, which was just as powerful as abuse and so he fed them, gave them fresh clothing, emptied their toilet, well toilet bucket to me more accurate, yuck! In essence, he looked after them."

"Well, he got that wrong didn't he?" said Brian.

"Yes, he did but who knows what would have happened if he had managed to keep Anne for longer. She did admit that she was warming to him but the opportunity to escape was just too good to ignore and so she stabbed him with the knife. The same knife he stabbed you with Brian."

"Right, okay, I can see what he was trying to do to prove his theory but surely that can't be the only reason why he kidnapped the two girls? I mean, why them?"

"That's the hard bit as he's not here to tell us but something the DCI told me makes me think that it was personal. According to the DCI, who interviewed his father, the Brigadier, William was married at one point but his obsession with psychology and his work at the university eventually resulted in the marriage ending. His estranged wife won full custody of their only daughter, Magdalene. Would it surprise you to know that Magdalene is of similar age to Lisa and Anne and not only that, both girls were very similar in appearance to Magdalene?"

"So you think that Lisa and Anne might have been a dress rehearsal for what he had in store for his own daughter? Capture her and then use what he had learned from his study of them to win over his daughter and form a relationship with her; a relationship which was denied him by the divorce?"

"It's only a theory," said Claire.

"He must have been off his head to think it would work!" said Brian.

Claire just nodded in agreement. "I think delusional is the correct psychological terminology."

Brian missed the intended irony in her correction. "It just goes to show you though that we would have identified him sooner rather than later, even without the DNA analysis."

"I know," said Claire. "Jim was a bit gutted that he didn't get to him before we did, but it proves what I always tell the team - it doesn't matter how small the lead, we must always check them out. After all, there is no such thing as perfect crime!"

Brian nodded in agreement. "Oh, I almost forgot to ask, how is your Dad doing?"

"He's much better thanks. They are keeping him in isolation for now until the tests come back. They think he's got coronavirus!"

"Really? That's not good!" said Brian. "I overheard some of the nurses talking about it. There's a real fear that it's going to spread quickly if the government doesn't do something about it quick."

"Yes, Peter says it's been all over the news. There's talk of a lockdown down south and possibly up here as well."

"I know," said Brian. Goodness knows how that will work for us trying to catch the bad guys?"

Claire hadn't really thought about it. She had been so pre-occupied with Peter's proposal and her dad's poor health that she hadn't really thought about much else over the last few days. Then she remembered the other reason why she had wanted to visit Brian.

"I almost forgot, I've other news to share and something to ask you", said Claire.

"Oh, and what's that?" asked Brian.

"Well, Peter and I have set a date to get married."

"Whoa, you've actually set a date? That was quick!"

"I know. Yes, in six weeks' time and if you are up for it, we would like you and Agnes to be our witnesses?"

He was stunned. "Yes, of course, but why me, I mean why us?"

Claire dodged the question. "Look it's no big deal. It's just going to be a small affair, local registration office, etc. Nothing fancy! So what do you say?"

"Claire, it would be an honour," said Brian who was beaming with delight.

The pair talked for another 10 minutes before Brian's nurse arrived to check his wound. Claire gave the big man a hug and went to leave the room.

"Oh, by the way Claire," said Brian. "You were wrong about one thing?"

"Was I?" she asked.

"Yes, remember you said that my unhealthy diet would kill me one day, well the doctor says that the opposite is the case."

"No way!" she said shaking her head in a slow exaggerated motion.

Brian was smiling. "Yes, he says that if I hadn't been so fat the knife would have gone deeper into my kidney and could have killed me. So there you go!"

Claire laughed, but she couldn't really argue with him. "Fair enough Brian, fair enough!"

About this book

Separating the facts from the fiction!

Spoiler alert!

Do not read any further if you have not read the story.

Readers of this story might be wondering if any of the information presented as facts within this book are real. For example, was William Wallace actually held in Dumbarton Castle by Menteith?

Well, Menteith was the Sheriff of Dumbarton at the time and it was widely thought that the only place he would have kept Wallace would have been in the castle but there is no hard evidence to say that this actually happened.

Was the medieval castle where Wallace was reportedly held in 1305 destroyed? True, it was burnt to the ground during a conduct.

Are there any hidden cells underneath the castle? Who knows? I made this bit up but would recommend a visit to Dumbarton Castle if you haven't been before. Perhaps you will be first to find the real dungeons!

Is the Keeper of the Castle a real title? Yes, Dumbarton Castle is one of three Royal Castles in Scotland and accordingly royal tradition suggests that the keys will be presented to the newly appointed monarch by the Keeper of the Castle.

Is the town of Dumbarton built on volcanic rock? Yes.

Can family history be traced through DNA? Yes.

Is the Fairbairn Theory vs Stockholm syndrome real? Yes.

Is the Professor's theory real? No, I made this bit up.

Residents of Dumbarton will recognise the controversial planning application to build another supermarket in the town. However, the outcome was different in reality and a new Lidl store was built on the waterfront.

Other titles by Andrew Hawthorne

There's no such thing as a Perfect Crime!
(DI Reading Book 1)

Claire Redding, a rising star within Police Scotland, is being fast tracked for greater things. Having played a key role in bringing down a major drugs gang in Glasgow, Claire is promoted to the position of Detective Inspector and transferred to 'L' Division in Dumbarton where she has to convince a well-established team of detectives that she is as good her reputation suggests. She is asked to solve a series of local burglaries which all have one thing in common; they all appear to be perfect crimes. DI Redding firmly believes that there is no such thing as a perfect crime and is determined to catch the elusive thief and further enhance her career prospects.

The pressure builds on the ambitious young DI when the burglaries are linked to a murder and local and national media ramp up interest in the case. It soon becomes crystal clear that the thief will not hesitate to kill anyone who gets in the way as the story races to a dramatic ending.

Who put that Spaceship on my school?!

(Illustrated by Elle Hunter)

This enchanting original children's story is about a young boy - Jack, who makes friends with a small alien called Bizak after he accidentally lands his spaceship on top of Jack's primary school in the Scottish town of Dumbarton.

Much to Jack's surprise Bizak asks for help and together they fly off into outer space on the adventure of a lifetime.

Printed in Great Britain
by Amazon

71899515R00119